The S
B

BY: Martin Gangley

Table of Contents

Chapter 1: A Perfect Beginning   4

Chapter 2: Cracks in the Foundation   15

Chapter 3: The Affair   26

Chapter 4: The Abuse Begins   38

Chapter 5: Seeking Help   48

Chapter 6: The Turning Point   58

Chapter 7: Therapy and False Hope   70

Chapter 8: Breaking Point   82

Chapter 9: The Decision to Leave   94

Chapter 10: Starting Over   104

Chapter 11: Legal Battles   114

Chapter 12: Healing and Reflection   126

Chapter 13: A New Beginning   136

Chapter 14: Escalating Danger   147

Chapter 15: A Mother's Betrayal   158

Chapter 16: The Car Accident   167

Chapter 17: Second Protection Order   179

Chapter 18: Trust Shattered   190

Chapter 19: Building a Safer Future   200

Chapter 1: A Perfect Beginning

The first time I saw her, she was laughing. A sound so pure and unrestrained, it cut through the thick Arizona heat and the chatter of the barbecue guests like a ray of sunshine. It hit me square in the chest, a jolt to a heart that had grown weary of cynicism and late nights poring over case files.

I was leaning against a weathered wooden fence, nursing a beer that was more sweat than alcohol at this point. It was supposed to be a night off, a chance to decompress after a grueling week tracking down a cyber-terrorist cell. But my mind kept drifting back to the blinking cursors, the encrypted messages, the looming threat of violence.

Then I saw her.

She was standing by the grill, a vibrant splash of yellow against the desert landscape. Her sun-kissed hair cascaded down her back, framing a face that radiated warmth and joy. She was engaged in an animated conversation with a group of women, her hands dancing in the air as she punctuated her words.

I found myself drawn to her like a moth to a flame. I wanted to know what had sparked that laughter, that pure, unadulterated joy. I wanted to bask in her light, if only for a moment.

Gathering my courage, I ambled over, beer in hand. "Mind if I join this lively discussion?" I asked, trying to sound casual despite the rapid thumping of my heart.

She turned, her smile widening as her eyes met mine. They were the color of emeralds, sparkling with amusement and a hint of something else – intrigue, perhaps?

"Not at all," she replied, her voice as bright and cheerful as her dress. "The more, the merrier!"

I introduced myself as Martin, a friend of the host. She told me her name was Rebekah, and that she had just moved to Phoenix a few weeks ago. We fell into easy conversation, the kind that feels like you're picking up where you left off with an old friend.

She was a preschool teacher, passionate about early childhood education. I told her about my work with the FBI's cyber division, careful to avoid the classified details that could get me in trouble. But even the sanitized version seemed to pique her interest.

"Wow, that sounds so intense," she said, her eyes wide with fascination. "I can't imagine dealing with cyber terrorists and stuff like that."

"It has its moments," I admitted, a wry grin tugging at my lips. "But it's not all bad. I get to wear a suit and carry a gun."

Her laughter bubbled up again, a delightful sound that chased away the last remnants of my work-induced stress.

"I bet you look very dashing in a suit," she teased.

"Only for you," I replied, unable to resist flirting with her.

As the night wore on, we moved from the grill to the dance floor, our laughter mingling with the music. We talked about everything under the sun: our families, our dreams, our fears. I learned that she was an artist in her spare time, creating stunning paintings and sculptures. She told me about her love for hiking and her obsession with spicy food.

I found myself opening up to her in a way I hadn't with anyone in a long time. There was something about her that made me feel safe, seen, understood. It was as if the universe had conspired to bring us together at this barbecue, in this moment.

As the party started to wind down, I walked her to her car, reluctant to let the night end. Under the glow of the streetlight, her eyes seemed to shimmer with an unspoken question.

"Would you like to go out sometime?" I asked, the words tumbling out before I could second-guess myself.

A radiant smile bloomed on her face, erasing any trace of doubt. "I'd love to," she replied.

We exchanged numbers, and I watched as she drove away, her taillights disappearing into the darkness. I stood there for a long moment, a warmth spreading through me that had nothing to do with the desert heat.

In the back of my mind, a tiny voice whispered a warning. It told me that I was getting ahead of myself, that I barely knew this woman. But I silenced that voice with a determined shake of my head. I had a feeling that Rebekah was different. That she was worth taking a chance on.

And as I turned and walked back towards my own car, a sense of anticipation filled me. I couldn't wait to see where this unexpected connection would lead.

―――――

The following week, Martin and Rebekah found themselves at a cozy Thai restaurant on 7th Street, their second date brimming with the same nervous excitement as their first. The warm, fragrant air filled with the aroma of lemongrass and chili, and the soft glow of paper lanterns created an intimate atmosphere.

Rebekah, her hair now flowing freely around her shoulders, wore a vibrant red top that accentuated her olive skin. Martin couldn't help but notice how the color matched the fiery spirit he was quickly discovering within her. He, in turn, had swapped his usual button-down for a more casual polo shirt, hoping to project a relaxed yet attentive demeanor.

"This place is amazing," Rebekah exclaimed, her eyes wide with delight as she took in the eclectic decor. "I love all the little details – the hand-painted murals, the intricately carved wooden screens."

"I knewyou'd appreciate it," Martin replied, a warm smile spreading across his face. "You have an artist's eye."

"Only an amateur one," Rebekah demurred, but the compliment clearly pleased her. "I dabble in painting and sculpting in my spare time. It's my way of de-stressing after a long day with the little ones."

"I'd love to see some of your work sometime," Martin said, genuinely interested.

"Maybe I'll bring you to my studio one day," Rebekah replied, her eyes twinkling with a hint of mischief.

They ordered a feast of spicy curries, stir-fries, and noodle dishes, sharing bites and laughing as they discovered a mutual love for fiery cuisine. The conversation flowed easily, punctuated by bursts of laughter and moments of shared intimacy.

"So, tell me more about your childhood," Martin prompted, eager to learn more about the woman who had captivated him.

Rebekah's smile softened as she recounted growing up in a small town in Ohio, surrounded by cornfields and friendly faces. She spoke of her close-knit family, her passion for art, and her early struggles with anxiety and depression.

Martin listened intently, his heart aching for the young girl who had faced such challenges. He found himself drawn to her vulnerability, her strength in the face of adversity.

"You're incredibly resilient," he said, reaching across the table to take her hand. "I admire that about you."

Rebekah's eyes met his, a flicker of gratitude in their depths. "Thank you," she whispered. "I've had to be."

In turn, Martin shared stories of his own upbringing. He spoke of his strict military father, his rebellious teenage years, and the trauma he had endured during his deployment in Afghanistan. He described his journey towards healing through therapy and his newfound purpose in helping others overcome their own demons.

Rebekah listened with empathy and understanding, her hand tightening around his. There was a depth to their connection that transcended the usual first-date pleasantries. They were two souls who had weathered their own storms, drawn together by a shared yearning for connection and healing.

As the night drew to a close, they strolled through the bustling streets of downtown Phoenix, hand in hand. The air was alive with the sounds of laughter, music, and the distant hum of traffic.

"I had a wonderful time," Rebekah said, her voice soft and sincere.

"Me too," Martin echoed. "You're amazing, Rebekah."

They paused under a streetlamp, the soft light casting a warm glow on their faces. Martin cupped Rebekah's cheek in his hand, his thumb gently tracing the outline of her lips.

"Can I kiss you?" he asked, his voice barely a whisper.

Rebekah nodded, her eyes closing as she leaned into him. Their lips met in a tender kiss, a gentle exploration of newfound affection. It was a kiss filled with promise, a kiss that hinted at the depth of feeling that was already blossoming between them.

As they parted, Rebekah rested her forehead against Martin's chest, her heart thrumming in unison with his.

"I have a feeling this is the beginning of something special," she murmured.

Martin wrapped his arms around her, holding her close. "I hope so," he whispered, his lips brushing against her hair.

They stood there for a long moment, lost in the embrace of their newfound love. The city lights twinkled around them, a backdrop to their budding romance. In that moment, they were oblivious to the challenges that lay ahead, the storms that would test their love. All that mattered was the here and now, the undeniable connection that had drawn them together and the promise of a future filled with love and laughter.

The drive to Sedona was a blur of desert landscapes, their hands intertwined on the center console as Rebekah's laughter filled the car. Martin had planned the surprise getaway meticulously, ensuring every detail was perfect, from the quaint bed and breakfast nestled among the red rocks to the curated itinerary of hikes and local attractions.

As they entered Sedona, the majestic red rock formations loomed over them, a testament to nature's artistry. Rebekah's eyes widened with awe, her fingers tightening around Martin's. They checked into their room, a cozy haven with exposed wooden beams, a crackling fireplace, and a private balcony overlooking the breathtaking scenery.

"It's absolutely perfect," Rebekah whispered, her voice filled with wonder as she explored their temporary abode.

"Not as perfect as you," Martin replied, his eyes twinkling with affection.

They spent the first day exploring the town, meandering through art galleries, sampling local delicacies, and soaking in the vibrant atmosphere. As the sun dipped below the horizon, casting long shadows across the landscape, they retreated to their balcony, a bottle of local wine in hand.

The air was crisp and cool, the silence punctuated only by the chirping of crickets and the gentle rustling of leaves. Rebekah rested her head on Martin's shoulder, her fingers tracing patterns on his arm.

"This is the most romantic place I've ever been," she sighed, her voice filled with contentment.

"Not quite as romantic as being with you," Martin whispered, his lips brushing against her hair.

They shared stories, dreams, and fears, their conversation weaving a tapestry of intimacy and understanding. Rebekah confided in Martin about her anxieties, the nightmares that sometimes plagued her sleep, and the lingering doubts she harbored about her self-worth.

Martin listened patiently, his heart aching for her. He offered words of comfort and reassurance, his voice steady and unwavering.

"You are strong, Rebekah," he said, his eyes meeting hers. "You are beautiful, and you are worthy of love."

His words washed over her like a soothing balm, easing the tension in her shoulders, the tightness in her chest. In that moment, she felt truly seen, truly understood.

As the night deepened, they moved inside, the fire crackling merrily in the hearth. They curled up on the plush sofa, their bodies intertwined, the warmth of their embrace a refuge from the cool desert air.

Their kisses grew more passionate, their touch more urgent. They shed their clothes, their bodies a symphony of desire and vulnerability. Their lovemaking was a dance of surrender and trust, their souls entwined as their bodies moved in perfect rhythm.

In the aftermath, they lay tangled in each other's arms, their breathing slow and steady. Rebekah traced the contours of Martin's face, her fingers lingering on his lips.

"I've never felt so connected to someone before," she murmured, her voice thick with emotion. "I feel like I can tell you anything, be anything with you."

"I feel the same way," Martin replied, his voice husky with sleep. "You're my safe haven, Rebekah. My home."

The following morning, they awoke to the golden rays of sunrise streaming through the window. They made love again, slow and tender, their bodies moving in perfect harmony. Afterwards, they lingered in bed, their fingers intertwined, their conversation peppered with laughter and whispered promises.

As they stood on their balcony, watching the sun rise over the majestic red rocks, Martin turned to Rebekah, his eyes filled with an emotion she had never seen before.

"I love you, Rebekah," he said, the words spilling from his lips with a sincerity that took her breath away.

Rebekah's heart swelled with joy, tears welling up in her eyes. "I love you too, Martin," she replied, her voice trembling with emotion.

They spent the rest of their weekend exploring Sedona, their love for each other growing with each passing moment. They hiked to the top of Cathedral Rock, where they shared a kiss as the sun dipped below the horizon, painting the sky with a kaleidoscope of colors. They dined at a romantic restaurant, their laughter echoing through the candlelit room.

As they drove back to Phoenix, their hearts full of love and hope, they couldn't have imagined the challenges that lay ahead. They were blissfully unaware of the storms that would test their love, the demons that would threaten to tear them apart. But for now, in this perfect bubble of happiness, they were content to simply be together, their love a beacon of light in a world filled with darkness.

Chapter 2: Cracks in the Foundation

The idyllic honeymoon phase of Martin and Rebekah's relationship gradually gave way to the rhythms of everyday life. As they settled into their shared apartment in Casa Grande, the initial euphoria began to fade, replaced by a more subdued reality. Martin, ever the observant therapist, noticed subtle shifts in Rebekah's demeanor, a dimming of the vibrant light that had initially drawn him to her.

One evening, as they sat on their balcony watching the sunset, Martin reached for Rebekah's hand. It felt cold and clammy in his.

"Everything okay?" he asked, concern lacing his voice.

Rebekah shrugged, her gaze fixed on the horizon. "Just tired," she murmured.

Martin studied her face, searching for the spark that usually danced in her eyes. It was absent, replaced by a dullness that tugged at his heart. He remembered the woman who had captivated him at the barbecue, the woman whose laughter had filled every corner of their shared space. That woman seemed a distant memory now.

In the weeks that followed, Martin noticed a pattern emerging. Rebekah's once infectious energy seemed to wane with each passing day. She spent hours staring blankly at the TV, her face devoid of emotion. The vibrant art projects she had once poured her heart into lay untouched in the corner of their spare room.

Even their conversations, once filled with laughter and shared dreams, had become strained and monosyllabic. Martin would try to engage Rebekah in conversation, but she would often respond with vague answers or simply shrug him off.

One night, as they lay in bed, Martin reached out to touch Rebekah's arm. She flinched, her body tensing up.

"Sorry," she mumbled, turning away from him.

Martin sighed, a knot of worry tightening in his stomach. He had tried talking to Rebekah about her withdrawal, but she always brushed it off, insisting she was just tired or stressed from work. But Martin knew it was more than that. He could sense a darkness creeping into her soul, a shadow that threatened to extinguish her light.

He decided to approach the issue more directly.

"Rebekah," he began, his voice gentle but firm. "I'm worried about you. You haven't been yourself lately."

Rebekah turned to face him, her eyes filled with a mixture of sadness and defiance. "I'm fine, Martin," she snapped. "Just leave me alone."

Martin reached out to stroke her hair, but she swatted his hand away. "Don't touch me," she hissed.

Hurt and confused, Martin retreated. He knew that pushing her would only make things worse. But he couldn't ignore the growing unease in his gut, the feeling that something was terribly wrong.

He decided to consult with a colleague, a therapist who specialized in mood disorders. After describing Rebekah's symptoms, the therapist suggested that she might be experiencing depression.

Martin felt a wave of relief wash over him. At least now he had a name for the darkness that was consuming his beloved. But he also knew that depression was a complex and often debilitating illness. He would need to be patient, understanding, and supportive.

That night, as Rebekah lay asleep beside him, Martin made a silent vow. He would do everything in his power to help her through this. He would be her rock, her anchor, her guiding light. He would not let the darkness win.

The next morning, Martin woke up to find Rebekah gone. A note on the kitchen table read:

"Gone for a walk. Need some air. Be back soon."

Martin's heart sank. He knew that Rebekah's walks were often a way for her to escape her demons, to find solace in the solitude of nature. But he also knew that she was vulnerable out there, alone with her thoughts.

He quickly got dressed and set out to find her. As he walked through the quiet streets of Casa Grande, his mind raced with worry. He prayed that he would find her safe and sound, that he would be able to bring her back into the light.

He found her sitting on a bench in a small park, her head buried in her hands. He sat down beside her, his arm wrapping around her shoulders. She didn't resist.

"I'm here for you, Rebekah," he whispered, his voice filled with love and concern. "We'll get through this together."

Rebekah leaned into him, her body shaking with silent sobs. Martin held her close, his heart filled with a mixture of sadness and determination. He knew that their journey would be long and arduous, but he was determined to see it through. He would not let the darkness steal away the woman he loved.

———

A few weeks later, the tension that had been simmering beneath the surface of their relationship finally erupted during a seemingly trivial argument about burnt toast. Martin had accidentally left the bread in the toaster for a few seconds too long, resulting in a charred and smoking mess.

"Seriously?" Rebekah snapped, her voice sharp and accusatory as she slammed her hand down on the kitchen counter. "Can't you even make toast without screwing it up?"

Martin flinched, taken aback by the vehemence of her reaction. "It was an accident," he said calmly, trying to diffuse the situation. "I'll make you another slice."

"Forget it," Rebekah retorted, her eyes flashing with anger. "I've lost my appetite."

She stormed out of the kitchen, leaving Martin staring at the burnt toast in bewilderment. He had never seen her this angry over something so insignificant.

Later that evening, as they sat down for dinner, the tension hung heavy in the air. Martin tried to initiate conversation, but Rebekah remained silent, her jaw clenched, her eyes fixed on her plate.

"Rebekah, please talk to me," Martin pleaded, reaching out to touch her hand.

She pulled her hand away, her voice icy. "What's there to talk about? You obviously don't care about my feelings."

"That's not true," Martin protested. "I just don't understand why you're so upset about the toast."

"It's not about the toast, you idiot!" Rebekah exploded, her voice rising to a shrill pitch. "It's about your constant carelessness, your complete disregard for my needs."

Martin stared at her, stunned by her outburst. He had always been attentive and caring, always striving to make her happy. He couldn't understand where this anger was coming from.

"Rebekah, please," he said softly. "I'm not perfect, but I love you. I want to make this work."

Rebekah scoffed, her eyes narrowed with contempt. "Love? Is that what you call it? You're suffocating me, Martin. You're controlling, and you're always trying to fix me. I'm not broken, damn it!" Martin felt a pang of hurt in his chest. He had never intended to control or suffocate her. He simply wanted to help, to support her through whatever she was going through.

"I'm just trying to understand," he said, his voice barely a whisper.

"You'll never understand," Rebekah retorted, her voice dripping with venom. "You're too wrapped up in your own perfect little world to see what's really going on."

She stood up abruptly, her chair scraping against the floor. "I'm going for a walk," she announced, grabbing her jacket and slamming the door behind her.

Martin sat alone at the table, staring at his untouched plate of food. He felt a deep sense of sadness and confusion. He didn't recognize the woman who had just lashed out at him. The Rebekah he knew was kind, compassionate, and loving. Where had that woman gone?

He tried to rationalize her behavior, blaming it on stress, exhaustion, or maybe even hormones. But deep down, he knew it was more than that. There was a darkness brewing within Rebekah, a darkness that he didn't understand and couldn't control.

As he washed the dishes, his mind raced with questions. What had happened to the woman he had fallen in love with? Was there any hope of salvaging their relationship? Or was this the beginning of the end?

The uncertainty gnawed at him, a constant reminder of the fragility of love and the destructive power of unresolved pain. He knew that he couldn't ignore the cracks that were appearing in their foundation. He had to find a way to reach Rebekah, to help her heal, before it was too late.

————

Martin sat alone in the living room, the silence amplifying the anxious thrumming in his ears. The argument had left him raw and unsettled. His gaze drifted to the bedroom door, behind which Rebekah had retreated in a storm of anger and accusations. He wrestled with a mix of emotions:

hurt, confusion, and a gnawing worry that burrowed deeper with each passing moment.

Unable to shake off the disquiet, he rose from the couch, his footsteps hesitant as he approached their bedroom. The door was slightly ajar, a sliver of light escaping into the darkened hallway. He paused, his hand hovering over the doorknob, a wave of uncertainty washing over him. Was this an intrusion? Was he crossing a boundary he shouldn't? Yet, the urgency to understand, to bridge the widening chasm between them, compelled him forward.

He pushed the door open gently, the hinges creaking softly in the quiet room. Rebekah lay curled up on the bed, her back to him, her shoulders rising and falling in shallow breaths. He hesitated, debating whether to wake her, but decided against it. Instead, his eyes scanned the room, seeking any clue that might shed light on the darkness that seemed to have enveloped her.

His gaze fell upon the nightstand, the drawers slightly ajar. Curiosity piqued, he moved closer, his fingers brushing against the smooth wood. The bottom drawer yielded easily, revealing a jumble of personal items: lotions, a hairbrush, a worn paperback novel. And then, nestled in the back corner, he saw it.

A small, orange prescription bottle.

His heart skipped a beat as he reached for it, his fingers trembling slightly. The label read "Sertraline," a common antidepressant. A wave of emotions crashed over him - shock, sadness, and a renewed sense of urgency. So his instincts had been right. The darkness wasn't just stress or exhaustion. It was something deeper, something that required professional help.

He placed the bottle back in the drawer, his mind racing. Should he confront Rebekah now? Or wait until she was in a calmer state? He decided on the latter. This was not a conversation to be rushed or forced. It required a delicate touch, a safe space for her to open up.

The next morning, as they sat at the breakfast table, an awkward silence hung between them. The remnants of the previous night's argument lingered in the air like a bitter aftertaste. Martin steeled himself, took a deep breath, and reached across the table to take Rebekah's hand.

"Rebekah," he began, his voice soft and gentle, "I found something in your drawer last night."

Her head snapped up, her eyes widening with alarm. "What are you talking about?"

"The medication," Martin said, choosing his words carefully. "The Sertraline."

Rebekah's face paled, her hand instinctively withdrawing from his. "It's nothing," she mumbled, her voice barely audible. "Just something for my...stress."

Martin's heart ached at the obvious lie. "Rebekah," he said, his voice filled with concern, "I know you're going through a tough time. I'm here for you, whatever it is. But you don't have to go through it alone."

She averted her gaze, her shoulders slumping. "I don't need your pity," she muttered, her voice thick with bitterness.

"It's not pity, Rebekah," Martin insisted. "It's love. I care about you. I want to help you."

She remained silent, her body rigid with tension.

"Please talk to me," Martin pleaded, his voice cracking with emotion. "Tell me what's going on. We can get through this together."

Rebekah finally looked up, her eyes filled with a mixture of shame and defiance. "You wouldn't understand," she said, her voice barely a whisper.

"Try me," Martin urged, his hand reaching out to hers once more.

She hesitated, then slowly, haltingly, began to open up. She spoke of the darkness that had been clouding her mind, the overwhelming sadness that made it difficult to get out of bed in the morning. She described the racing thoughts that kept her awake at night, the self-doubt that gnawed at her confidence.

Martin listened intently, his heart breaking for her. He understood now why she had been withdrawing from him, why her once vibrant spirit had dimmed. He also realized that he had been naive to think he could fix her on his own. This was a battle she needed to fight with professional help.

"I'm so glad you told me," he said, his voice filled with relief and gratitude. "I'm here for you, every step of the way. We'll get through this together."

Rebekah nodded, a single tear rolling down her cheek. She was not alone in this fight. She had Martin by her side, and that was all that mattered. Or so she thought.

But as the days turned into weeks, Martin would learn that her illness was far more complex than simple depression, and the shadows lurking in Rebekah's past were far darker than he could

Chapter 3: The Affair

Weeks after their romantic Sedona getaway, an undercurrent of unease began to taint the once-blissful atmosphere of Martin and Rebekah's home. Rebekah's withdrawal intensified, replaced by an erratic energy that swung between bursts of manic activity and sullen isolation. Martin tried to be supportive, attributing her behavior to stress and the medication she was on. However, a nagging sense of doubt gnawed at him, whispering insidious possibilities in his ear.

One evening, as Rebekah showered, her phone buzzed with a text message. Martin, usually respectful of her privacy, found himself unable to resist the urge to glance at the screen. His heart pounded in his chest as he read the message:

"Can't wait to see you tonight, beautiful. You looked stunning in that dress ;) - Alex."

His blood ran cold. A name he didn't recognize, a message dripping with intimacy. He felt a sickening lurch in his stomach as a wave of betrayal washed over him. Could it be? Could the woman he loved, the woman he had bared his soul to, be deceiving him?

He replaced the phone where he found it, his hands shaking. He retreated to the living room, his mind racing with a torrent of questions and accusations. He paced back and forth, the silence of the apartment amplifying the deafening roar in his ears.

When Rebekah emerged from the bathroom, her hair damp and a towel wrapped around her body, she found Martin sitting on the couch, his face pale and drawn.

"What's wrong?" she asked, a flicker of concern in her eyes.

Martin looked up, his gaze unwavering. "Who's Alex?" he asked, his voice barely a whisper.

Rebekah froze, her face draining of color. "What are you talking about?" she stammered, her eyes darting nervously.

Martin held up her phone, his finger pointing to the incriminating text message. "This Alex," he said, his voice hardening. "The one who can't wait to see you tonight."

Rebekah's composure crumbled. Her eyes filled with tears, her body trembling as she sank onto the edge of the bed.

"I'm so sorry," she sobbed, her voice barely audible. "I didn't mean to hurt you."

Martin felt a surge of anger, his fists clenching involuntarily. "Didn't mean to hurt me?" he repeated, his voice laced with incredulity. "How could you do this to me, Rebekah? After everything we've been through, after all the promises we made..."

His voice trailed off, choked with emotion. He couldn't believe that the woman he loved, the woman he had trusted implicitly, could betray him in such a cruel and callous way.

buried her face in her hands, her sobs racking her body. "I know I messed up," she cried. "I'm so sorry. I don't know what came over me."

Martin sat beside her, his anger subsiding into a numbing sadness. He gently lifted her chin, forcing her to meet his gaze.

"Why, Rebekah?" he asked, his voice heavy with pain. "Why did you do this?"

Rebekah's eyes were red and swollen, her face etched with guilt and shame. "I don't know," she whispered. "I was feeling lost, empty. I needed something, anything, to make me feel alive again."

"And you found that in Alex?" Martin asked, his voice laced with bitterness.

Rebekah shook her head. "No," she admitted. "It was a mistake. I was lonely, and he made me feel wanted. But it doesn't mean anything. I love you, Martin. You're the only one I want."

Martin's heart ached at her words. He wanted to believe her, to forgive her, but the betrayal cut too deep. He felt like a fool, a pawn in her game of deception.

"I don't know what to do," he said, his voice filled with despair. "I love you, but I don't know if I can ever trust you again."

Rebekah reached out to him, her eyes pleading for forgiveness.

"Please, Martin," she begged. "Give me another chance. I promise

I'll never hurt you again."

Martin looked into her eyes, searching for a glimmer of the woman he had fallen in love with. But all he saw was the wreckage of their shattered trust.

He stood up, his body heavy with the weight of his decision. "I need some time to think," he said, his voice barely above a whisper. He turned and walked out of the room, leaving Rebekah alone with her tears and her guilt.

———

The apartment, once a sanctuary of shared dreams and budding love, now felt like a suffocating prison. The air crackled with unspoken accusations, every shadow seeming to harbor a lurking betrayal. Martin stood rigid, his knuckles white as he gripped the back of a chair, his eyes locked on Rebekah, who sat huddled on the edge of the bed, her shoulders shaking with silent sobs.

"Tell me it's not true," he pleaded, his voice hoarse with barely restrained anger.

Rebekah finally looked up, her eyes red and swollen, her face a mask of guilt and shame. "I'm so sorry," she choked out, the words barely audible. "I didn't mean for it to happen."

Her words were like a match to gasoline, igniting the fury that had been simmering within Martin. "Didn't mean for it to happen?" he spat, his voice dripping with sarcasm. "So, it just magically occurred? You just happened to fall into another man's arms?" cowered under his gaze, her voice barely a whisper. "It wasn't like that. It started as a friendship, a way to escape...my thoughts."

"Escape?" Martin scoffed, his voice rising. "You escape into another man's bed? Is that how you deal with your problems now?"

Rebekah flinched, her eyes welling up with fresh tears. "No, it wasn't like that. It was...a mistake. A terrible mistake."

"A mistake?" Martin's voice echoed through the apartment, the word dripping with scorn. "A mistake that you repeated, over and over again. How many times, Rebekah? How many times did you betray our love, our trust?"

Rebekah remained silent, her body trembling as she clutched a pillow to her chest.

"Answer me!" Martin demanded, his voice booming through the room.

"I don't know," she whispered, her voice barely audible. "It doesn't matter. It was wrong, and I'm so sorry."

Martin stared at her, his heart hardening with each passing second. The woman he had adored, the woman he had believed was his soulmate, was a stranger now, a deceitful stranger who had shattered his world into a million pieces.

"How could you do this to me?" he asked, his voice raw with pain. "After everything we've been through, after all the promises we made..."

He trailed off, unable to finish the sentence. The hurt was too immense, the betrayal too deep. He felt like a fool, a naive idiot who had been blinded by love.

Rebekah reached out to him, her eyes pleading for forgiveness. "Please, Martin," she begged. "Don't give up on us. I know I messed up, but I love you. You're the only one I want."

Martin recoiled, pulling his hand away as if her touch burned him. "Love?" he spat, the word laced with venom. "You have a twisted way of showing it."

He paced the room, his anger simmering just below the surface. "Do you even realize what you've done?" he asked, his voice trembling with rage. "You've destroyed everything we had. Our trust, our intimacy, our future..."

Rebekah buried her face in her hands, her sobs growing louder. "I know," she wailed. "I'm so sorry. I hate myself for what I've done."

Her words did little to appease Martin's anger. He felt betrayed, humiliated, and utterly lost. The foundation of their relationship, once built on love and trust, had crumbled beneath the weight of her infidelity.

"I don't know if I can ever forgive you," he said, his voice hollow and empty. "I don't know if I even want to."

looked up, her eyes filled with despair. "Please, Martin," she pleaded. "Give me another chance. I promise I'll change. I'll do anything to make it right."

Martin stared at her, his heart torn in two. He wanted to believe her, to give their love another chance. But the pain was too raw, the wound too fresh. He knew that even if he forgave her, the doubt would always linger, poisoning their relationship.

He took a deep breath, steeling himself for what he had to say. "I need some time," he said, his voice barely a whisper. "I need time to think, to process all of this."

He turned and walked out of the bedroom, leaving Rebekah alone with her shattered promises and broken dreams. As he closed the door behind him, he felt a wave of nausea wash over him. The life he had envisioned with Rebekah, the future they had planned together, seemed like a distant mirage, a cruel illusion shattered by the harsh reality of betrayal.

———

The air hung heavy with tension as Martin fled the stifling confines of their apartment. The desert night, usually a soothing balm for his troubled mind, offered no comfort tonight. Each step he took on the cracked pavement felt like a blow to his heart, each breath a struggle against the suffocating grief that threatened to consume him.

He found himself at the doorstep of his closest friend, Alex – a fellow FBI agent, his confidant, and his voice of reason in times of turmoil. Without waiting for an invitation, Martin pushed open the unlocked door and stumbled inside.

Alex was in the kitchen, nursing a glass of whiskey, his brow furrowed in concentration as he stared out the window. He turned at the sound of Martin's entrance, his eyes widening in surprise.

"Martin? What are you doing here at this hour?"

Martin didn't answer. He simply collapsed onto the nearest chair, his head in his hands, his shoulders shaking with suppressed sobs.

Alex, alarmed by his friend's state, quickly poured him a glass of whiskey and sat down beside him. "Hey, what's wrong? Talk to me."

Martin took a deep breath, trying to compose himself. "She cheated on me," he choked out, the words barely audible. "Rebekah...she's been having an affair."

Alex's expression hardened. "Are you sure?"

Martin nodded, unable to meet his friend's eyes. "I saw the messages. There's no denying it."

A heavy silence descended upon the room, broken only by the ticking of the clock on the wall. Alex reached out and clapped a hand on Martin's shoulder, his grip firm and reassuring.

"I'm so sorry, man," he said, his voice filled with empathy. "This is a tough one."

Martin took a long swig of whiskey, the burning liquid offering a momentary distraction from the pain. "I don't know what to do," he confessed, his voice raw with emotion. "I love her, but I can't believe she would do this to me. After everything we've been through..."

His voice trailed off, choked with tears. Alex sat in silence, allowing his friend the space to grieve. He knew there were no words that could adequately express the pain and betrayal Martin was feeling.

After a while, Martin spoke again, his voice steadier now. "I don't know if I can ever trust her again. How can I build a future with someone who's capable of such deceit?"

Alex nodded, understanding the turmoil his friend was experiencing. "Trust is the foundation of any relationship," he said. "Once it's broken, it's incredibly difficult to rebuild."

Martin sighed, his shoulders slumping. "I know," he said. "But I love her, Alex. I can't just throw away everything we have."

"Love is a powerful thing," Alex acknowledged. "But it's not always enough. Sometimes, you have to love yourself enough to walk away from a toxic situation."

Martin fell silent, contemplating his friend's words. He knew that Alex was right, but the thought of losing Rebekah was unbearable. He had invested so much of himself in their relationship, in their shared dreams of a future together.

"I don't know what to do," he repeated, his voice filled with despair.

"There's no easy answer, Martin," Alex said. "You have to do what feels right for you. But whatever you decide, I'm here for you. You're not alone in this."

Martin nodded, grateful for his friend's unwavering support. He stayed at Alex's place that night, the two men talking long into the night, sharing stories, memories, and fears.

As the first light of dawn crept through the window, Martin felt a sense of clarity settle over him. He realized that while he loved Rebekah, he couldn't allow her betrayal to define him. He couldn't sacrifice his own happiness and well-being for a love that was built on lies.

He made a decision. He would confront Rebekah one last time, give her a chance to explain herself, to show genuine remorse. But if he didn't see the change he needed, he would walk away, no matter how much it hurt.

As he left Alex's house, a new resolve filled him. This was not the end, but a new beginning. He would pick up the pieces of his shattered heart and move forward, stronger and wiser for the experience. He would find a love that was true, a love that would cherish and respect him, a love that would never betray his trust.

Chapter 4: The Abuse Begins

The days following the revelation of Rebekah's infidelity were marked by a fragile truce. A tense quietude settled over their apartment, replacing the easy laughter and warmth that had once defined their relationship. Martin, wrestling with his hurt and confusion, attempted to maintain a semblance of normalcy. He went to work, cooked meals, and tried to engage Rebekah in conversation. But his efforts were met with a wall of silence, her eyes clouded with a distant, haunted look.

One evening, as Martin prepared dinner, he accidentally knocked over a spice jar, sending a cloud of paprika billowing through the air. Rebekah, who had been silently reading on the couch, jumped up, her eyes blazing with fury.

"For God's sake, Martin!" she shrieked, her voice sharp and accusatory. "Can't you do anything right?"

Martin flinched, his hand instinctively reaching to wipe away the spilled spice. "I'm sorry," he mumbled, his voice barely a whisper. "It was an accident."

"Accident?" Rebekah scoffed, her lips twisted in a sneer. "You're always so clumsy, always making a mess. Can't you be more careful?"

Her words stung, a venomous barb piercing his heart. He had always been a bit clumsy, a trait Rebekah had once found endearing. Now, it seemed to be a source of constant irritation.

The incident was just the beginning. In the days that followed, Rebekah's criticism grew sharper, her barbs more pointed. She nitpicked at his every move, his clothes, his cooking, his work. No matter how hard he tried to please her, nothing seemed to be good enough.

"You're always working late," she would complain, her voice dripping with accusation. "Do you even care about this family?"

Or she would say, "You're such a slob, Martin. Why can't you keep this place tidy?"

Martin found himself walking on eggshells, constantly second-guessing his actions, afraid of triggering another outburst. He started to doubt himself, his confidence eroding under the weight of her constant criticism.

Not content with verbal attacks, Rebekah began to isolate him from his friends and family. She would make snide remarks about his friends, accusing them of being a bad influence. She would cancel plans at the last minute, citing vague excuses. She would even intercept phone calls from his mother, claiming that he was too busy to talk.

Martin felt increasingly alone and isolated, his world shrinking until it revolved solely around Rebekah and her volatile moods. He longed for the camaraderie of his friends, the warmth of his family, but he was afraid to defy Rebekah's wishes, fearing her wrath.

One evening, as he was getting ready to go out with his colleagues for a drink, Rebekah blocked the doorway, her arms crossed, her expression defiant.

"Where do you think you're going?" she demanded.

"I'm just going out with some friends," Martin replied, trying to keep his voice calm.

"You're not going anywhere," Rebekah said, her voice laced with venom. "You're staying here with me."

"Rebekah, I need to go," Martin said, his patience wearing thin. "I haven't seen my friends in weeks."

"I don't care," Rebekah retorted. "You're not leaving this house."

Martin tried to reason with her, but she remained unmoved. He could see the anger simmering in her eyes, the threat of violence lurking beneath the surface. He knew that if he pushed her, she would erupt, and he didn't want to risk a scene in front of his friends.

Reluctantly, he agreed to stay home, his heart heavy with resentment and frustration. As he watched his friends leave without him, he felt a wave of despair wash over him. He was trapped in a prison of Rebekah's making, a prison of isolation and emotional abuse. He didn't know how much longer he could endure it. _____

The air hung thick with tension, a palpable force that seemed to press down on Martin's chest. The aborted night out with his friends had left a bitter taste in his mouth, fueling the resentment that simmered beneath his forced smile. Rebekah, sensing his unease, moved about the kitchen with a restless energy, her movements jerky and erratic.

"You're not even going to try to be happy about it?" she asked, her voice sharp as she slammed a pan onto the stove. "I stayed home for you, and this is the thanks I get?"

Martin took a deep breath, trying to calm the storm brewing inside him. "I'm grateful, Rebekah," he said, his voice tight. "But I would have appreciated a heads up, not a confrontation in front of my friends."

Rebekah whirled around, her eyes blazing. "Oh, so now I'm the bad guy?" she spat. "I'm the one who's always controlling and manipulative, right?"

"I didn't say that," Martin protested, holding up his hands in a placating gesture.

"But you were thinking it," Rebekah accused, her voice rising with each word. "You always think the worst of me. You never trust me."

"That's not fair," Martin countered. "I trust you, but I also need my own space, my own friends."

Rebekah scoffed, a humorless sound that grated on Martin's nerves. "Friends? Those losers? They're nothing but a bunch of drunken idiots."

Martin's jaw clenched. "Don't talk about my friends like that," he warned, his voice dangerously low.

The atmosphere in the kitchen crackled with electricity, the tension so thick you could cut it with a knife. Rebekah stalked towards him, her eyes narrowed into slits.

"Or what?" she challenged, her voice a venomous hiss. "What are you going to do about it, Martin? Are you going to hit me?"

Her words were a calculated jab, a deliberate attempt to provoke him. Martin knew he shouldn't rise to the bait, but his patience had worn thin.

"Don't be ridiculous," he retorted, his voice laced with frustration. "I would never hit you."

Rebekah laughed, a cold, hollow sound that sent chills down Martin's spine. "Oh really?" she sneered. "You're just like all the other men. You think you're so much better than us, but you're all the same."

She stepped closer, her face inches from his. "You're weak," she whispered, her breath hot against his skin. "Pathetic. A disappointment."

Her words struck a chord deep within Martin, a primal rage igniting in his gut. But before he could react, Rebekah's hand flashed out, striking him hard across the face.

The sound of the slap echoed through the kitchen, a sharp, shocking report that shattered the illusion of control Martin had been clinging to. He staggered back, his hand instinctively flying to his stinging cheek.

Rebekah stood before him, her chest heaving, her eyes wild with a manic energy. "Don't you ever talk back to me again," she snarled, her voice dripping with menace.

Martin stared at her, shock and disbelief warring with the rage that pulsed through his veins. He had never been hit before, not by anyone, and certainly not by the woman he loved.

Tears welled up in his eyes, a mixture of pain, humiliation, and a profound sense of betrayal. He stumbled back, his hand still cradling his cheek, his voice barely a whisper.

"Rebekah..."

But she was already turning away, a triumphant smirk playing on her lips. She sauntered out of the kitchen, leaving Martin standing there, alone and shattered.

He collapsed onto a chair, his head in his hands, his body wracked with sobs. He felt like a broken man, his pride and dignity in tatters. He had never felt so small, so insignificant, so utterly powerless.

As the tears flowed freely, he knew that this was a turning point. The woman he had fallen in love with, the woman he had believed was his soulmate, had revealed a dark and violent side to her nature. He didn't know if he could ever trust her again, if he could ever look at her the same way.

The foundation of their relationship had been irrevocably cracked. The question now was whether it could be repaired, or whether it would crumble completely, leaving nothing but dust and ashes in its wake.

———

The following day, the sting of Rebekah's slap still lingered on Martin's cheek, a physical reminder of the emotional turmoil that now gripped their home. Each glance in the mirror brought a fresh wave of humiliation and confusion. How could the woman he loved, the woman who had once been his haven, inflict such pain?

Unable to bear the weight of his secret alone, Martin reached for his phone, his fingers trembling as he dialed his mother's number. It rang twice before her familiar voice answered, warm and comforting as always.

"Martin, honey, how are you?" she asked.

He hesitated, the words catching in his throat. "Mom, I need to talk to you," he finally managed, his voice thick with emotion.

"Of course, sweetie. What's wrong?"

Martin took a deep breath, steeling himself for the confession he was about to make. "Rebekah...she hit me."

There was a stunned silence on the other end of the line, then his mother's voice, sharp with alarm. "Hit you? What do you mean?"

Martin recounted the events of the previous night, the argument, the insults, the stinging slap. His voice wavered as he described the pain and humiliation he had felt.

"Oh, Martin," his mother sighed, her voice heavy with sadness. "I'm so sorry."

"I don't know what to do," Martin confessed, his voice cracking. "I love her, Mom, but I can't live like this."

"You don't have to," his mother said firmly. "No one deserves to be treated that way. You need to get out of there, Martin. For your own safety, and for the sake of your future."

Martin's grip on the phone tightened. "But...I can't just leave her. She's sick, Mom. She needs help."

"I know she's struggling, Martin," his mother said gently. "But that doesn't excuse her behavior. You can't let her abuse you like this. It's not healthy, and it's not right."

Martin remained silent, his mind a battleground of conflicting emotions. He knew his mother was right, but a part of him still clung to the hope that Rebekah would change, that their love could overcome this darkness.

"I think she's going to start therapy," he said, his voice barely a whisper. "Maybe that will help."

"Therapy is a good start," his mother conceded. "But you can't rely on it to fix everything. You need to protect yourself, Martin. You need to set boundaries."

Martin sighed, his shoulders slumping. "I know, Mom," he said.
"But it's not that easy. I love her. I made a commitment to her."

"Love isn't supposed to hurt like this, Martin," his mother reminded him. "You deserve to be happy, to be treated with respect. You don't have to sacrifice your own well-being for someone who can't even control their own anger."

Martin closed his eyes, his mother's words echoing in his mind. He knew she was right, but the thought of leaving Rebekah filled him with a profound sense of loss. He had invested so much of himself in their relationship, in their shared dreams of a future together.

"I just need some time," he said, his voice barely audible. "I need to think."

"Take all the time you need, sweetie," his mother said. "But please, promise me you'll be careful. Don't let her manipulate you or guilt you into staying. You deserve better than this."

Martin promised his mother he would be careful, but as he hung up the phone, a wave of doubt washed over him. He wanted to believe that Rebekah could change, that their love was strong enough to withstand this storm. But deep down, he knew that the road ahead would be long and arduous, filled with pain and uncertainty.

The first step was acknowledging the truth of his situation. Rebekah had become abusive, and he couldn't ignore it any longer. He had to prioritize his own safety and well-being, even if it meant walking away from the woman he loved.

It was a decision that would change the course of his life, a decision that would break his heart and shatter his dreams. But it was a decision he had to make, for himself and for the future he deserved.

Chapter 5: Seeking Help

The sterile glow of the fluorescent lights seemed to magnify the starkness of the community center's basement room. Martin sat hunched in a folding chair, his hands clasped tightly in his lap. The air hummed with nervous energy, the silence punctuated only by the occasional cough or the rustle of papers.

He scanned the faces of the other men in the room, a motley crew of varying ages and backgrounds. Some looked hardened and stoic, their eyes betraying a deep-seated pain. Others wore a mask of forced bravado, their smiles brittle and unconvincing. A few, like Martin, appeared lost and bewildered, their expressions etched with a mixture of shame and confusion.

This was his first time attending a support group for victims of domestic violence. He had hesitated for weeks, wrestling with his pride and his fear of being judged. But the isolation had become unbearable, the weight of his secret too heavy to carry alone. He needed to talk to someone, anyone, who understood what he was going through.

The group leader, a middle-aged woman with kind eyes and a soothing voice, began the meeting with a brief introduction. She explained the purpose of the group, the importance of confidentiality, and the guidelines for respectful communication.

Then, she invited the men to share their stories.

One by one, they spoke, their voices trembling at times, their eyes filled with tears. They spoke of the physical and emotional abuse they had endured, the manipulation and control that had stripped them of their dignity and self-worth. They spoke of the fear, the shame, the isolation that had become their constant companions.

Martin listened intently, his heart aching with each story. He heard echoes of his own experiences in their words, the same patterns of abuse, the same cycles of hope and despair. It was both horrifying and comforting to know that he wasn't alone.

A burly man named Tony spoke of how his wife had belittled him for years, chipping away at his self-esteem until he felt like a worthless shell of a man.

A soft-spoken man named David shared how his partner had isolated him from his family and friends, controlling his every move until he felt trapped and suffocated.

A young man named Jake described the physical violence he had endured, the bruises and broken bones that were a testament to his partner's rage.

As Martin listened to their stories, a sense of camaraderie began to form. These men, despite their differences, shared a common bond of pain and resilience. They had all been victims, but they were not defined by their victimhood. They were survivors, men who had found the strength to seek help, to speak their truth, to reclaim their lives.

When it was Martin's turn to speak, he hesitated, his heart pounding in his chest. He had never shared his story with anyone before, not even his mother. But as he looked around the room, at the faces of the men who had opened their hearts to him, he felt a surge of courage.

He cleared his throat and began to speak, his voice trembling at first. He told them about Rebekah, about their whirlwind romance, their dreams of a future together. He described the subtle changes in her behavior, the escalating emotional abuse, the first instance of physical violence.

As he spoke, the room fell silent. The men listened with rapt attention, their faces etched with empathy and understanding. They nodded their heads in agreement, their eyes conveying a shared experience of pain and betrayal.

When Martin finished, there was a moment of silence, then a chorus of voices offering support and encouragement.

"You're not alone, brother," Tony said, his voice gruff but kind.

"We've all been there," David added, his eyes filled with compassion.

"You're strong, Martin," Jake said, his voice filled with admiration. "You'll get through this."

Martin felt a wave of warmth wash over him, a sense of belonging he hadn't felt in a long time. He had finally found a safe space where he could be vulnerable, where he could share his pain without fear of judgment.

As the meeting drew to a close, Martin felt a glimmer of hope flicker within him. He knew that he had a long road ahead of him, a journey of healing and self-discovery. But he also knew that he was not alone. He had found a community of survivors, men who understood his pain and offered him strength.

As he left the community center, the weight on his shoulders felt a little lighter. He had taken the first step towards healing, the first step towards reclaiming his life from the clutches of abuse. The road ahead would be challenging, but he was no longer walking it alone. He had found his tribe, his brothers in arms, and together, they would find their way out of the darkness.

———

The echoes of the support group's shared experiences resonated within Martin, strengthening his resolve. Armed with newfound validation and a flicker of hope, he returned home, determined to confront Rebekah about her abusive behavior.

He found her in the living room, curled up on the couch, a half-finished glass of wine on the coffee table. The TV flickered with the muted glow of a late-night infomercial, casting long shadows across her face. She looked up as he entered, her expression a mixture of defiance and vulnerability.

Martin took a deep breath, his heart pounding in his chest. "Rebekah," he began, his voice soft but steady, "we need to talk."

Rebekah's eyes narrowed. "What about?" she asked, her voice clipped.

"About what happened last night," Martin said, referring to the events of the support group. "I talked to some people who are going through similar experiences, and it helped me realize that what you're doing is not okay."

Rebekah scoffed, a cold, mocking laugh escaping her lips. "Oh, really? And what do these experts have to say about our little spat?"

Martin ignored her sarcasm, choosing his words carefully. "They said that emotional abuse is just as damaging as physical abuse. It's about control, manipulation, and power. And that's what you've been doing to me, Rebekah. You've been belittling me, isolating me, and making me doubt myself."

Rebekah's face hardened, her eyes blazing with anger. "Don't you dare lecture me, Martin. You have no idea what I'm going through. I'm the one who's struggling here, remember?"

"I know you're struggling," Martin said, his voice softening. "And I want to help you. But you can't keep hurting me like this. It's not fair, and it's not right."

Rebekah rose from the couch, her movements sharp and agitated. "You're always the victim, aren't you?" she spat. "Always blaming me for everything. Well, guess what? You're not perfect either. You're always working late, you never listen to me, and you're always trying to fix me. Maybe I wouldn't be so angry if you weren't such a disappointment."

Martin felt a wave of frustration wash over him. He had expected her to be defensive, but her complete denial and deflection of blame caught him off guard.

"I'm not trying to fix you, Rebekah," he said, his voice rising in frustration. "I'm trying to help you. I'm trying to understand what you're going through so we can get through this together."

Rebekah threw her hands up in exasperation. "You're impossible!" she exclaimed. "You always twist my words, make me out to be the villain. I'm the one who needs help, not you."

Martin took a deep breath, trying to regain his composure. He reminded himself that he was dealing with someone who was hurting, someone who was lashing out from a place of pain.

"I know you're hurting, Rebekah," he said, his voice softening again. "But hurting me isn't going to make things better. We need to find a healthy way to communicate, to work through our issues together."

Rebekah turned away, her shoulders shaking. Martin could hear the muffled sound of her sobs. He moved towards her, his arms outstretched, wanting to comfort her. But she recoiled from his touch.

"Don't," she said, her voice barely a whisper. "Just leave me alone."

Martin hesitated, unsure of what to do. He didn't want to leave her in this state, but he also didn't want to push her further. He decided to give her some space, hoping that she would calm down and be open to talking later.

He retreated to the bedroom, his heart heavy with sadness and uncertainty. He had hoped that confronting Rebekah would be a turning point, a catalyst for change. But it seemed to have only pushed her further away.

He lay awake for hours that night, staring at the ceiling, his mind a jumble of conflicting thoughts and emotions. He loved Rebekah, but he couldn't allow himself to be her punching bag. He had to protect himself, to set boundaries, even if it meant risking the end of their relationship.

As the first light of dawn crept through the window, Martin made a decision. He would not give up on Rebekah, but he would no longer tolerate her abuse. He would seek professional help for himself, learn how to navigate this toxic situation, and protect himself from further harm. He would fight for his own well-being, even if it meant facing the painful reality that his love for Rebekah might not be enough to save their relationship.

The following day, a heavy fog of dread hung over Martin as he sat at his desk at the FBI field office. The usually familiar hum of computer servers and the chatter of his colleagues felt distant and muffled, as if he were observing the world through a thick pane of glass. His mind replayed the events of the previous night, each scene a painful reminder of the unraveling of his once-happy home.

Rebekah's words, sharp and accusatory, echoed in his ears, fueling a growing sense of despair. He had always believed in the power of love to heal, to mend even the deepest wounds. But now, he questioned if their love was strong enough to withstand the destructive force that had taken hold of Rebekah.

As he stared blankly at his computer screen, a wave of nausea washed over him. He couldn't bear the thought of returning home, of facing another evening filled with tension and hostility. He needed an escape, a moment of clarity away from the suffocating atmosphere of their apartment.

He grabbed his jacket and car keys, slipping out of the office unnoticed. The cool desert air hit him like a slap, momentarily clearing his head. He got into his car and drove aimlessly, the familiar streets blurring into a kaleidoscope of colors as he grappled with his conflicting emotions.

He knew he couldn't continue like this. He couldn't allow himself to be a victim, to be subjected to Rebekah's escalating abuse. But the thought of leaving her, of breaking up their family, filled him with a profound sense of guilt and failure.

He pulled over to the side of the road, his hands gripping the steering wheel until his knuckles turned white. He closed his eyes, his mind racing with a torrent of thoughts. He needed help, guidance, a way out of this labyrinth of pain and confusion.

A sudden thought struck him, a spark of hope in the darkness that had engulfed him. He reached for his phone and dialed a number he had been reluctant to call until now.

"Hello, this is Robert Johnson," a voice answered on the other end of the line. "How can I help you?"

Martin hesitated, his throat tightening with emotion. "Mr.
Johnson, my name is Martin Reed. I need...I need your help."

Robert Johnson was a family law attorney, a name that had been recommended to Martin by a colleague at the FBI. He was known for his expertise in handling complex divorce cases, especially those involving domestic violence.

Martin explained his situation, his voice trembling at times as he recounted the emotional and physical abuse he had endured at the hands of his wife. He spoke of his fear for his own safety, his concern for the well-being of their unborn child.

Johnson listened patiently, his voice calm and reassuring. "Mr. Reed," he said, "I understand this is a difficult time for you. But you're not alone. Many men experience domestic violence, and it's important to know that you have options."

Martin felt a wave of relief wash over him. Just hearing those words, knowing that someone understood and believed him, was a validation he desperately needed.

Johnson explained the legal process of obtaining a restraining order, the steps involved in filing for divorce, and the potential for seeking sole custody of their child. He outlined the challenges and the potential risks, but also the possibility of a brighter future for Martin and his child.

As Martin listened, he felt a glimmer of hope ignite within him. He realized that he didn't have to endure this abuse any longer. He had the power to protect himself, to create a safe and healthy environment for his child.

The decision to leave Rebekah would not be easy. It would be a painful and messy process, filled with heartbreak and uncertainty. But as he hung up the phone, Martin knew that it was the right decision. He had to prioritize his own safety and the well-being of his child. He had to break free from the cycle of abuse and reclaim his life.

He took a deep breath, the first step on a new path, a path towards healing and freedom. The road ahead would be long and arduous, but he was determined to walk it, one step at a time, until he reached the light at the end of the tunnel.

Chapter 6: The Turning Point

The following weekend, Martin's in-laws, Helen and Richard, came to visit. Helen, Rebekah's mother, had been growing increasingly concerned about her daughter's behavior and wanted to check on her. Martin, caught between his desire to protect Rebekah and his growing fear for his and Mariah's safety, had reluctantly agreed to the visit.

The tension was palpable from the moment Helen and Richard stepped into the apartment. Rebekah, in a rare display of composure, greeted them with forced smiles and polite conversation. But beneath the veneer of normalcy, Martin could sense the storm brewing within her.

Dinner was a strained affair, filled with awkward silences and stilted conversation. Helen, ever the perceptive mother, picked up on the tension between her daughter and son-in-law. She exchanged concerned glances with Richard, who remained stoically silent, his eyes darting between Martin and Rebekah.

After dinner, as Helen helped Rebekah clear the table, Martin retreated to the living room to play with Mariah. The two-year-old squealed with delight as her father chased her around the coffee table, their laughter momentarily dispelling the oppressive atmosphere.

But the respite was short-lived.

A sudden crash from the kitchen shattered the tranquility. Martin and Mariah froze, their laughter dying in their throats. A moment later, Rebekah stormed into the living room, her face contorted with rage, a glint of steel in her hand.

"You!" she screamed, brandishing a kitchen knife. "You're ruining my life!"

Martin's blood ran cold. He instinctively scooped up Mariah, shielding her small body with his own. "Rebekah, calm down," he pleaded, his voice trembling. "What's wrong?"

"You're what's wrong!" she shrieked, lunging towards him with the knife. "You're the reason I'm so miserable. You're holding me back!"

Martin dodged her attack, his heart pounding in his chest. He could feel Mariah trembling in his arms, her tiny body pressed against his.

"Rebekah, please," he begged. "Think about Mariah. This isn't you."

But Rebekah was beyond reason. Her eyes blazed with an unhinged fury, her voice a guttural growl.

"You're a liar!" she screamed. "A manipulator! You've never loved me. You just want to control me, to destroy me!"

She lunged again, the knife flashing dangerously close to Martin's face. He managed to deflect her blow, but the blade sliced through his shirt, leaving a thin line of blood on his chest.

Helen and Richard rushed into the room, their faces etched with horror.

"Rebekah!" Helen cried, her voice filled with shock and disbelief.
"What are you doing?"

Rebekah whirled around, her eyes wild. "Stay out of this, Mother!" she snarled. "This is between me and him."

Richard stepped forward, his voice booming with authority. "Put the knife down, Rebekah. Now."

Rebekah hesitated, her eyes darting between her parents and Martin. The knife wavered in her hand, then clattered to the floor.

Helen rushed to Martin's side, her eyes filled with concern. "Are you alright, dear?" she asked, her hand hovering over his wound.

Martin nodded, his gaze fixed on Rebekah. He could see the madness in her eyes, the utter lack of remorse. A cold dread settled over him, a realization that this was not the woman he had married, the woman he had loved.

This was a stranger, a dangerous stranger, and she was a threat to him and their child.

In that moment, something within Martin shifted. The last vestiges of hope, the lingering belief that Rebekah could be saved, evaporated into the stifling air. He knew now, with absolute certainty, that he had to protect Mariah, even if it meant leaving the woman he had once vowed to love and cherish.

As the police arrived, summoned by a frantic Helen, Martin held Mariah close, his heart filled with a newfound resolve. He would not let fear dictate his actions. He would fight for his daughter, for her safety and well-being. He would not rest until she was safe from the clutches of the monster that Rebekah had become.

———

The wail of the siren pierced the tense silence of the apartment, a harsh counterpoint to Mariah's whimpered cries. Martin clutched his daughter close, his heart pounding in his chest as he watched the police officers escort Rebekah out of the apartment. Her mother, Helen, stood by the door, her face etched with a mixture of shock and despair.

As the front door closed behind them, a heavy silence settled over the room. Martin looked down at Mariah, her tear-streaked face buried in his shoulder. He gently stroked her hair, murmuring words of comfort, his own voice trembling with suppressed emotion.

Helen approached him, her eyes filled with concern. "Martin, are you alright?" she asked, her voice barely a whisper.

He nodded, unable to speak past the lump in his throat. He glanced back at the door, a wave of nausea washing over him as he imagined Rebekah's rage-filled face, the glint of the knife in her hand.

"We need to get out of here," he said, his voice barely audible. "I need to take Mariah somewhere safe."

Helen nodded, her expression grim. "You're right," she said. "Let's go to my house. You can stay there as long as you need to."

Martin gratefully accepted her offer, gathering Mariah's things and carrying her out to his car. As they drove through the dark desert night, he glanced at his daughter in the rearview mirror. She had fallen asleep, her small body curled up in her car seat, her face peaceful in slumber.

The sight of her innocence, her vulnerability, filled Martin with a fierce determination. He would protect her, no matter what. He would not allow Rebekah's madness to touch her, to taint her childhood with fear and violence.

When they arrived at Helen's house, she welcomed them with open arms. She took Mariah in her arms, cooing softly as she carried her to the guest room. Martin followed, his heart heavy with gratitude for his mother-in-law's unwavering support.

"I don't know what I would do without you," he said, his voice thick with emotion.

Helen smiled sadly, her hand reaching out to squeeze his. "You're family, Martin," she said. "And family looks out for each other."

They sat down at the kitchen table, a pot of tea steaming between them. Martin poured his heart out to Helen, recounting the events of the past few months, the escalating abuse, the fear, the despair. He spoke of his attempts to reason with Rebekah, his hopes for therapy, his growing realization that the situation was beyond his control.

Helen listened patiently, her eyes filled with compassion and understanding. She had seen the warning signs in Rebekah's behavior, the subtle shifts in mood, the outbursts of anger. But she had never imagined that her daughter was capable of such violence.

"I'm so sorry, Martin," she said, her voice thick with emotion. "I never wanted this for you, for Mariah."

Martin reached out and took her hand in his. "I know," he said. "But I'm grateful for your support. I don't know what I would do without you."

Helen squeezed his hand, her eyes filled with determination. "We'll get through this together," she said. "We'll protect Mariah, no matter what."

They spent the rest of the evening talking, their conversation a lifeline in the stormy sea of Martin's emotions. Helen shared stories of Rebekah's childhood, her struggles with anxiety and depression, her tendency to lash out when overwhelmed.

Martin listened intently, pieces of the puzzle falling into place. He began to understand the root of Rebekah's anger, the deep-seated pain that had festered and grown until it consumed her.

As the night wore on, Martin felt a sense of clarity settle over him. He knew that he had to take action, to protect Mariah from further harm. He would seek legal counsel, file for a restraining order, and fight for sole custody of his daughter.

He also knew that he couldn't do it alone. He needed the support of his family and friends, the guidance of professionals, the strength of his own resolve. But most importantly, he needed to believe in himself, to trust his instincts, and to never give up on the fight for his daughter's safety and happiness.

As he drifted off to sleep that night, Martin felt a flicker of hope ignite within him. It was a small flame, easily extinguished, but it was enough to keep him going. He would face the challenges ahead with courage and determination, knowing that he was not alone in this battle. He had his mother-in-law, his friends, and the unwavering love for his daughter to guide him through the darkness.

———

The sterile atmosphere of the courthouse did little to calm Martin's nerves. The echoing footsteps and hushed whispers in the marbled halls only amplified his sense of isolation. He clutched a manila folder filled with evidence: photos of his bruised cheek, copies of threatening text messages from Rebekah, and a detailed account of the night she pulled a knife on him.

His hands trembled slightly as he pushed open the heavy wooden door to the family court clerk's office. A middle-aged woman with a kind face looked up from her computer, her expression a mixture of curiosity and concern.

"Can I help you?" she asked.

Martin swallowed hard, his voice barely a whisper. "I...I need to file for a restraining order."

The woman nodded sympathetically, her eyes softening. "Come on in," she said, gesturing towards a small, private room. "Let's talk."

Martin followed her into the room, his heart pounding in his chest. He sat down at the table, the folder clutched tightly in his hands. The woman sat opposite him, her gaze steady and reassuring.

"My name is Ms. Davis," she said. "I'm here to help you through this process. Can you tell me what happened?"

Martin took a deep breath, steeling himself for the painful retelling of his ordeal. He recounted the escalating abuse, the emotional manipulation, the physical violence. He described the fear that had become a constant companion, the sleepless nights spent worrying about his and Mariah's safety.

Ms. Davis listened intently, her pen scribbling furiously on a notepad. She asked clarifying questions, her voice gentle but firm. Martin answered honestly, his voice wavering at times as he relived the traumatic events.

As he spoke, a wave of sadness washed over him. He had loved Rebekah, had believed in their future together. But now, faced with the stark reality of her abusive behavior, he realized that love was not enough. He had to protect himself and his daughter, even if it meant severing ties with the woman he had once cherished.

When Martin finished his story, Ms. Davis looked up, her eyes filled with compassion. "Mr. Reed," she said, "I believe you. You're not alone in this. Many men experience domestic violence, and it's important to remember that it's never your fault."

Her words were like a balm to Martin's wounded soul. He had been carrying the weight of shame and self-blame for so long, convinced that he was somehow responsible for Rebekah's behavior. But now, hearing those words from a stranger, a professional who dealt with these situations every day, he felt a burden lifted from his shoulders.

Ms. Davis explained the legal process of obtaining a restraining order. She detailed the steps involved, the potential challenges, and the resources available to him. She assured him that he was not alone, that there were people who could help him through this difficult time.

Martin listened intently, his mind racing with questions. He wanted to know how long the process would take, what his chances of success were, and what the impact would be on his and Mariah's lives.

Ms. Davis answered his questions patiently, providing him with the information he needed to make an informed decision. She stressed the importance of safety, urging him to take precautions and seek support from friends and family.

As Martin signed the paperwork, his hand trembling slightly, he felt a mix of relief and sadness. He knew that this was a necessary step towards protecting himself and his daughter, but he also mourned   the   loss   of the life he had once envisioned with
Rebekah.

He left the courthouse feeling emotionally drained but strangely empowered. He had taken the first step towards reclaiming his life, towards breaking free from the cycle of abuse. The road ahead would be long and uncertain, but he knew that he was not alone. He had the law on his side, the support of his loved ones, and the unwavering determination to protect his child.

As he drove away from the courthouse, he glanced in the rearview mirror at Mariah, who was fast asleep in her car seat. A wave of fierce protectiveness washed over him. He would do whatever it took to keep her safe, to shield her from the darkness that had threatened to consume their family.

He knew that this was just the beginning of a long and arduous journey. But he was ready to face it head-on, armed with the knowledge that he was not a victim, but a survivor. He would rise above the pain and the fear, and he would emerge stronger and more resilient than ever before.

Chapter 7: Therapy and False Hope

The sterile, beige walls of the therapist's office seemed to suffocate Martin as he sat on the plush, floral-patterned couch, the scent of lavender incense thick in the air. Rebekah sat beside him, her posture rigid, her arms crossed defensively across her chest. The tension between them was palpable, a dense fog that hung heavy in the otherwise serene space.

Dr. Amelia Grant, a woman with a warm smile and a reassuring demeanor, sat opposite them, her notepad resting on her lap. She had a reputation for being one of the best marriage counselors in Casa Grande, her approach a blend of empathy and pragmatism. Martin had pinned his hopes on her, desperate for a solution to the unraveling tapestry of their marriage.

"Thank you both for coming today," Dr. Grant began, her voice calm and measured. "I understand that you've been going through a difficult time."

Rebekah let out a derisive snort, her eyes rolling towards the ceiling. "Difficult is an understatement," she muttered under her breath.

Martin shot her a warning glance, but she ignored him, her gaze fixed on a painting of a serene mountain landscape on the wall behind Dr. Grant.

Dr. Grant cleared her throat, unfazed by Rebekah's hostility. "I'd like to start by having each of you share your perspective on what's been happening in your relationship."

Martin took a deep breath, his hands trembling slightly as he began to speak. He recounted the escalating abuse, the verbal attacks, the physical violence, and the growing sense of fear and isolation he felt. He spoke of his attempts to communicate his concerns, his pleas for Rebekah to seek help. His voice cracked with emotion as he described the incident with the knife, the terror he had felt for both himself and Mariah.

Dr. Grant listened intently, her eyes occasionally darting to Rebekah, who remained stubbornly silent, her gaze still fixed on the painting.

When Martin finished, Dr. Grant turned to Rebekah. "Rebekah," she said gently, "would you like to share your perspective?"

Rebekah finally looked away from the painting, her eyes narrowed with defiance. "There's nothing to share," she retorted. "He's exaggerating everything. He's always been overly sensitive."

Martin's jaw clenched, his anger rising. He opened his mouth to protest, but Dr. Grant held up a hand, silencing him.

"Rebekah," she said, her voice firm but compassionate, "I understand that you're feeling defensive. But it's important for us to hear your side of the story as well."

Rebekah hesitated, her eyes darting nervously around the room.
Finally, she spoke, her voice barely a whisper.

"He's not perfect, you know," she said, her tone accusatory. "He works too much, he neglects me, he doesn't appreciate me. He's always criticizing me, always trying to change me."

Martin listened in disbelief, his heart sinking. Rebekah was twisting the truth, painting herself as the victim. He wanted to scream, to defend himself, but he held his tongue, knowing that it would only escalate the situation.

Dr. Grant intervened, her voice calm and steady. "Rebekah," she said, "I understand that you're feeling frustrated and unheard. But it's important to communicate your needs in a healthy way, without resorting to insults or accusations."

Rebekah scoffed, her eyes flashing with contempt. "You're taking his side," she accused, her voice rising. "You don't understand what it's like to be married to him."

Dr. Grant remained unruffled, her voice unwavering. "My role is not to take sides," she explained. "My role is to help you both communicate more effectively and find solutions to the problems in your relationship. But in order to do that, you both need to be willing to listen to each other, to acknowledge each other's feelings."

Rebekah crossed her arms, her body language radiating defiance. "I've heard enough," she said, rising from the couch. "This is a waste of time."

She stormed out of the office, leaving Martin and Dr. Grant in stunned silence. Martin buried his face in his hands, a wave of despair washing over him. He had hoped that therapy would be a turning point, a chance to mend the fractures in their relationship. But Rebekah's resistance and manipulation had only served to deepen the divide between them.

He looked up at Dr. Grant, his eyes filled with a mixture of sadness and defeat. "I don't know what to do," he confessed, his voice barely a whisper.

Dr. Grant reached out and placed a comforting hand on his arm. "Don't give up hope, Martin," she said. "Change is possible, but it takes time and effort from both parties. If Rebekah is unwilling to engage in the process, then you need to focus on protecting yourself and your daughter."

Martin nodded, a glimmer of determination returning to his eyes. He knew that he had a long and difficult road ahead of him, but he was no longer alone. He had the support of a therapist who understood the complexities of his situation, and he had the strength of his own conviction to guide him.

———

The following week, Martin returned to Dr. Grant's office alone, his heart heavy with the weight of Rebekah's refusal to engage in therapy. He recounted the events of the previous session, his voice laced with frustration and despair.

"I don't know what to do," he confessed, running a hand through his hair. "I feel like I'm losing her, Dr. Grant. I'm losing the woman I love."

Dr. Grant listened patiently, her eyes filled with empathy. "I understand your pain, Martin," she said. "But it's important to remember that you can't force someone to change if they're not ready. You can only control your own actions and reactions."

She paused, her gaze thoughtful. "However," she continued, "I believe there's still hope. Rebekah may be resistant to therapy right now, but that doesn't mean she won't come around eventually. Sometimes, people need time to process their emotions, to confront their demons."

Martin nodded, a glimmer of hope flickering in his eyes. "I hope you're right," he said.

"In the meantime," Dr. Grant advised, "focus on taking care of yourself. Set healthy boundaries, communicate your needs clearly, and don't be afraid to seek support from your loved ones."

Martin took her words to heart, determined to follow her advice. He started spending more time with his friends and family, seeking solace in their company and their unwavering support. He also began practicing mindfulness and meditation, techniques he had learned during his own therapy sessions to manage his stress and anxiety.

A few weeks later, Rebekah surprised Martin by agreeing to attend another therapy session. She arrived at Dr. Grant's office looking somber and withdrawn, her eyes downcast, her shoulders hunched.

Martin's heart pounded with a mixture of hope and trepidation. He wanted to believe that this was a turning point, that Rebekah was finally ready to face her demons and work towards healing their relationship.

The session began with an awkward silence, the tension in the room palpable. Dr. Grant, sensing the emotional charge, gently guided the conversation, encouraging both Martin and Rebekah to express their feelings openly and honestly.

As the session progressed, something unexpected happened. Rebekah's facade of defiance crumbled, replaced by a vulnerability that Martin had not seen in weeks. She spoke of her childhood trauma, her struggles with mental illness, and the overwhelming fear that had driven her to seek solace in another man's arms.

She confessed to the pain she had caused Martin, the betrayal she had inflicted on their marriage. Her voice cracked with emotion as she apologized for her hurtful words and actions.

"I know I've been horrible," she sobbed, her shoulders shaking. "I'm so sorry, Martin. I don't know why I do these things. I don't know how to stop."

Martin listened intently, his heart aching for her. He saw the desperation in her eyes, the genuine remorse in her voice. He wanted to believe her, to forgive her, to embrace her with open arms.

He reached out and took her hand, his thumb gently stroking her knuckles. "I love you, Rebekah," he said, his voice thick with emotion. "I want to help you get through this. But you have to want to change, to heal. You have to be willing to do the work."

Rebekah nodded, her tears flowing freely. "I do," she whispered. "I want to change. I want to be better, for you, for Mariah, for myself."

In that moment, a glimmer of hope ignited in Martin's heart. He saw a flicker of the woman he had fallen in love with, the woman who had once filled his life with joy and laughter.

He leaned forward and embraced her, his arms wrapped tightly around her trembling body. He held her close, whispering words of comfort and reassurance.

As they left Dr. Grant's office, hand in hand, Martin couldn't help but feel a cautious optimism. Perhaps this was the turning point they so desperately needed, the beginning of a new chapter in their relationship. He knew that the road ahead would be challenging, but he was willing to walk it with Rebekah, hand in hand, towards a future filled with healing and hope.

———

The days following Rebekah's apparent breakthrough in therapy were a whirlwind of cautious optimism for Martin. He clung to her promises of change like a lifeline, his heart buoyed by the hope of a brighter future. He noticed subtle shifts in her behavior – softer words, a gentler touch, a willingness to listen. He dared to believe that their love could conquer the darkness that had threatened to consume them.

One evening, as they sat down for dinner, Martin presented Rebekah with a small, velvet box. Her eyes widened with surprise as she opened it, revealing a delicate silver necklace with a pendant shaped like a heart.

"It's beautiful," she breathed, her fingers tracing the intricate design. "Thank you."

Martin smiled, his heart swelling with love. "It's a symbol of my love for you," he said, his voice thick with emotion. "A reminder that we can overcome anything, as long as we have each other."

Rebekah leaned in and kissed him, her lips soft and yielding. For a moment, the weight of the past few weeks seemed to lift, replaced by a fleeting sense of normalcy.

But the illusion of peace was short-lived.

As the weeks turned into months, Rebekah's promises of change proved to be empty. The tender moments were fleeting, quickly replaced by the familiar patterns of manipulation and control. The verbal barbs returned, sharper and more cutting than before.

"You're so predictable," she sneered one morning as Martin prepared for work. "Always rushing off to your precious job, leaving me to deal with everything here."

Or she would say, "You're so boring, Martin. I can't believe I ever married you."

The emotional abuse was a constant drip, eroding Martin's self-esteem, chipping away at his spirit. He tried to reason with her, to remind her of the progress they had made in therapy, but his words fell on deaf ears.

One evening, as they were arguing about household chores, Rebekah's anger boiled over. She grabbed a vase from the mantelpiece and hurled it at Martin, narrowly missing his head. He ducked instinctively, the shattered porcelain raining down around him.

"You're useless!" she screamed, her face contorted with rage. "I can't stand the sight of you!"

Martin stared at her, his heart pounding in his chest. He couldn't believe that this was the woman he had loved, the woman he had vowed to protect. The fear that had been simmering beneath the surface now bubbled up, a cold dread filling his veins.

He backed away slowly, his hands raised in a placating gesture. "Rebekah, please calm down," he said, his voice trembling. "Let's talk about this."

But Rebekah was beyond reason. She lunged at him, her nails raking down his face, leaving bloody trails in their wake. Martin tried to defend himself, to push her away, but she was relentless, her fury fueled by years of pent-up resentment and pain.

He finally managed to break free, his cheek stinging, his clothes torn. He retreated to the bedroom, locking the door behind him.

He could hear Rebekah pounding on the door, her screams echoing through the apartment.

He sat on the edge of the bed, his head in his hands, his body shaking with sobs. He felt like a broken man, his dreams shattered, his heart bleeding. He had tried everything to save their marriage, to help Rebekah, but it was clear that she was not ready to change.

The realization hit him like a punch to the gut. He had been living in a fantasy, a delusion that Rebekah could be the woman he had once loved. But the truth was staring him in the face, cold and harsh. She was not the woman he had married, the woman he had vowed to cherish.

He was married to a monster.

A monster who had stolen his joy, his peace, his very sense of self. He was a prisoner in his own home, trapped in a cycle of abuse that was slowly destroying him.

He knew he couldn't stay. He had to leave, for his own sanity, for his own survival. But the thought of leaving Rebekah, of abandoning her to her demons, filled him with a profound sense of guilt and despair.

He was torn, his heart a battleground of conflicting emotions. But as he lay in bed that night, staring at the ceiling, he knew that he had to make a choice. He had to choose between his own well-being and the hope of a love that might never be.

And as the first light of dawn crept through the window, Martin made his decision. He would leave. He would take

Mariah and run, far away from the toxic environment that was poisoning their lives. He would start over, build a new life, a life free from fear and pain.

It was a decision that would break his heart, but it was a decision he had to make. He had to save himself, and he had to save his daughter.

Chapter 8: Breaking Point

The apartment was a tinderbox, each passing day igniting new sparks of Rebekah's volatile rage. Her apologies and promises of change had become a cruel taunt, a twisted game she played to keep Martin trapped in her web of manipulation.

One evening, as Martin sat at the kitchen table, his head buried in a stack of bills, a chilling silence descended upon the room. He could feel Rebekah's eyes boring into his back, the intensity of her gaze a tangible force that raised the hairs on his arms.

He slowly turned, his heart pounding in his chest. Rebekah stood in the doorway, her face contorted in a mask of fury, her eyes blazing with a manic intensity.

"You're not even listening to me," she accused, her voice a venomous hiss. "I've been talking to you for the past five minutes, and you haven't even acknowledged me."

Martin sighed, a weariness settling over him. "I'm sorry, Rebekah," he said, his voice calm and measured. "I was focused on these bills. What did you say?"

His words only served to ignite her rage. "Oh, so now I'm boring you?" she sneered, taking a menacing step towards him. "I'm not interesting enough for you anymore?"

Martin pushed back his chair, his instincts screaming at him to get away. "Rebekah, please calm down," he pleaded, his voice trembling. "Let's not do this again."

But it was too late. Rebekah lunged at him, her fists flying. Martin raised his arms to protect himself, but her blows rained down on him, relentless and unforgiving. He felt the sharp sting of her nails raking down his face, the sickening thud of her fists connecting with his ribs.

He stumbled backward, trying to shield himself, but she followed, her attacks becoming more frenzied. She kicked at his legs, her boots leaving painful bruises on his shins. She grabbed his hair, yanking his head back with a vicious force.

Martin cried out in pain, his body wracked with sobs. He was no match for her rage, her strength fueled by years of pent-up frustration and resentment.

"Stop!" he begged, his voice barely a whisper. "Please, Rebekah, stop!"

But she didn't stop. She continued her assault, her punches and kicks raining down on him like a relentless storm. He curled into a ball on the floor, his arms wrapped around his head, trying to protect himself from the blows.

He could hear her screams, her curses, her threats. He could feel the warm trickle of blood on his face, the sharp pain in his ribs. But most of all, he felt a profound sense of terror, a sickening realization that he was utterly powerless in the face of her fury.

Finally, after what seemed like an eternity, the onslaught ceased. Rebekah stood over him, her chest heaving, her eyes wild with a manic energy. She spat on him, her voice dripping with contempt. "Worthless," she hissed. "You're nothing but a worthless piece of trash."

Then, she turned and walked away, leaving Martin crumpled on the floor, his body bruised and broken, his spirit shattered.

He lay there for a long time, his mind numb, his body aching. He felt like a shell of a man, stripped of his dignity, his pride, his very essence. He had never felt so vulnerable, so exposed, so utterly alone.

As he slowly picked himself up, the realization dawned on him. He could no longer pretend that this was just a rough patch, a temporary lapse in Rebekah's sanity. This was a pattern, a cycle of abuse that was only going to escalate.

He staggered to the bathroom, his reflection in the mirror a stark reminder of the violence he had endured. His face was bruised and swollen, his eyes bloodshot, his lip split. He looked like a stranger, a ghost of the man he once was.

As he splashed cold water on his face, a wave of nausea washed over him. He retched violently, his body heaving as he emptied the contents of his stomach into the sink.

When the nausea subsided, he leaned against the sink, his head in his hands, his body wracked with sobs. He had reached his breaking point. He could no longer endure the pain, the fear, the constant threat of violence. Hehad to get out, to protect himself, to save himself.

But how? How could he escape the clutches of the woman he loved, the woman who had once been his everything? How could he break free from this toxic cycle of abuse and reclaim his life?

The answer came to him in a blinding flash of clarity. He had to leave. He had to take Mariah and run, far away from the darkness that had consumed their home. He had to start over, build a new life, a life free from fear and pain.

He knew it wouldn't be easy. Rebekah would fight him every step of the way, using every weapon in her arsenal to keep him trapped in her web of manipulation. But he was determined. He would not let her win. He would fight for his freedom, for his daughter's safety, for the future they both deserved.

With a newfound resolve, Martin straightened his shoulders, wiped away his tears, and left the bathroom. He went to Mariah's room, where she slept peacefully, oblivious to the storm that had raged around her. He gently scooped her up in his arms, her tiny body warm and soft against his chest.

As he carried her out of the apartment, he made a silent vow. He would protect her, no matter what. He would never let anyone hurt her again. He would give her the life she deserved, a life filled with love, laughter, and safety.

This was his turning point, the moment he took back control of his destiny. And as he walked away from the apartment, his heart filled with a mixture of fear and determination, he knew that he would never look back.

———

The sterile, impersonal office of his therapist, once a source of solace, now felt like another battleground. Martin sat hunched on the familiar leather armchair, his gaze fixed on the abstract painting that hung on the wall opposite him. It was a chaotic swirl of colors and shapes, a fitting representation of the turmoil that raged within him.

Dr. Grant, his therapist, sat across from him, her expression a mask of professional concern. She had witnessed the gradual deterioration of Martin's spirit over the past few months, the toll that Rebekah's escalating abuse had taken on his mental and physical well-being.

"Martin," she began, her voice gentle but firm, "I'm deeply concerned about your safety. The situation at home seems to be worsening, and I'm worried that Rebekah's behavior is escalating."

Martin nodded, his voice barely a whisper. "It is," he confessed, his eyes filling with tears. "It's worse than ever before."

He recounted the latest incident, the brutal attack that had left him bruised and battered. He described the fear that now consumed him, the constant dread of what Rebekah might do next.

"I don't know how much more I can take," he admitted, his voice cracking with emotion. "I feel like I'm living in a war zone."

Dr. Grant listened intently, her brow furrowed with concern. She had seen countless cases of domestic violence in her career, but Martin's situation was particularly troubling. Rebekah's erratic behavior, coupled with her refusal to seek help, painted a bleak picture.

"Martin," she said, her voice grave, "I believe you are in a dangerous situation. Your safety, and the safety of your daughter, is paramount. I urge you to prioritize your well-being and consider leaving the marriage."

Martin's head snapped up, his eyes wide with surprise. "Leave?" he repeated, the word foreign and terrifying. "But...I love her. I can't just abandon her."

"Love is a complex emotion, Martin," Dr. Grant said gently. "It can blind us to the truth, make us believe that we can endure anything for the sake of the person we love. But love shouldn't hurt like this. It shouldn't leave you feeling scared and powerless."

Martin's shoulders slumped, his gaze falling to the floor. He knew she was right, but the thought of leaving Rebekah filled him with a profound sense of guilt and failure. He had vowed to love her through thick and thin, to stand by her side no matter what. But now, faced with the harsh reality of her abuse, he questioned if that vow was even possible to keep.

"I don't know what to do," he confessed, his voice choked with emotion. "I feel trapped, lost."

Dr. Grant leaned forward, her eyes filled with compassion. "Martin, you're not trapped," she said. "You have choices. You can choose to stay in this toxic environment, or you can choose to leave and create a safe and healthy life for yourself and your daughter."

She paused, letting her words sink in. "Leaving is not a sign of weakness," she continued. "It's a sign of strength, of self-love, of the courage to prioritize your own well-being. It's about taking back control of your life."

Martin listened intently, his mind racing with a torrent of thoughts. He had always been a protector, a fixer, someone who believed he could save others from their demons. But now, he realized that he couldn't save Rebekah. He could only save himself.

He looked up at Dr. Grant, his eyes filled with a newfound resolve. "You're right," he said, his voice steady. "I need to leave. I need to protect myself and my daughter."

Dr. Grant nodded, a glimmer of hope in her eyes. "That's a brave decision, Martin," she said. "I'm proud of you."

She handed him a list of resources, including domestic violence shelters, legal aid organizations, and support groups for men who had experienced abuse.

"Don't hesitate to reach out for help," she encouraged him. "You don't have to go through this alone."

Martin thanked her, his heart filled with gratitude for her guidance and support. He left her office feeling a strange mixture of sadness and liberation. He knew that the road ahead would be long and difficult, but he was no longer alone. He had a plan, a purpose, and a newfound determination to create a better life for himself and his daughter.

———

The apartment held its breath, each object seeming to bear witness to the shattered remnants of Martin's dreams. The once vibrant colors had faded into a dull, oppressive gray, mirroring the bleakness that had settled over his heart. He moved through the familiar rooms like a ghost, his footsteps barely disturbing the silence that clung to the air like a shroud.

He started in the bedroom, the scene of countless nights of passion and whispered promises, now tainted by violence and betrayal. He opened his dresser drawers, his fingers tracing the soft cotton of his shirts, the worn leather of his belts. Each item held a memory, a fragment of the life he had once shared with Rebekah.

He carefully folded his clothes, placing them into a suitcase. As he packed, a wave of grief washed over him, a mourning for the love that had been lost, the future that had been stolen. He paused, his hand hovering over a framed photograph of him and Rebekah on their wedding day. Their smiles radiated happiness, their eyes sparkling with hope. It was a cruel reminder of the life they had once shared, a life that now seemed like a distant, bittersweet dream.

He quickly set the photo aside, his resolve hardening. He couldn't allow himself to dwell on the past, on the fragments of a shattered illusion. He had to focus on the present, on the task at hand.

He moved to Mariah's room, the sight of her sleeping form a balm to his wounded soul. She lay curled up in her crib, her chubby cheeks flushed, her breath coming in soft, even puffs. He gently lifted her into his arms, her tiny body warm and trusting against his chest.

He kissed her forehead, a silent vow echoing in his heart. He would protect her, no matter what. He would give her the life she deserved, a life free from fear and pain.

He carried her to the living room, where he had already packed a small bag of her essentials. He placed her in her car seat, securing the straps with trembling hands. Then, he returned to the bedroom to finish packing.

As he moved through the apartment, he gathered the few remaining items he deemed essential: his laptop, his work documents, a few cherished books. He left behind the furniture, the appliances, the countless trinkets and mementos that had once filled their home with warmth and personality.

He paused in the doorway of the living room, taking one last look around. The emptiness of the space mirrored the emptiness in his heart. He had loved this apartment, had envisioned raising a family here, growing old with Rebekah within its walls. But those dreams were now nothing more than ashes scattered in the wind.

He turned and walked out the door, Mariah's car seat clutched tightly in his hand. He didn't look back, afraid that if he did, he might lose his resolve.

He drove through the deserted streets of Casa Grande, the headlights of his car cutting through the darkness. Mariah slept soundly in the backseat, oblivious to the life-altering journey they were embarking on.

Martin's mind raced with a mixture of emotions. He felt a sense of relief, a weight lifted from his shoulders, knowing that he had finally escaped the toxic environment that had been poisoning his soul. But he also felt a profound sadness, a grief for the loss of his marriage, the shattered dreams of a future with Rebekah.

He knew that the road ahead would be difficult. He would have to face legal battles, financial struggles, and the emotional turmoil of starting over. But he was determined to face those challenges head-on, armed with the knowledge that he was doing what was best for himself and his daughter.

As he drove towards his mother's house, a sanctuary of love and support, he made a silent vow. He would never look back. He would never allow himself to be drawn back into the destructive cycle of abuse. He would build a new life, a life filled with love, laughter, and peace.

He would never forget the pain and suffering he had endured, but he would not let it define him. He would use his experience to help others, to raise awareness about domestic violence, to offer hope and healing to those who had suffered in silence.

As the sun began to rise, casting a golden glow over the desert landscape, Martin arrived at his mother's house. He carried Mariah inside, her sleeping form nestled against his chest.

He knew that this was just the beginning of a long and arduous journey. But he also knew that he was not alone. He had the support of his family, his friends, and a newfound determination to create a better life for himself and his daughter.

He had reached his breaking point, but he had also found his strength. And as he looked down at his sleeping daughter, he knew that he would do whatever it took to protect her, to give her the life she deserved.

He would never look back.

Chapter 9: The Decision to Leave

The sterile white walls of the temporary apartment felt like a blank canvas, a stark contrast to the life Martin had left behind. The air hung heavy with the scent of fresh paint and disinfectant, a sterile mask over the lingering echoes of past tenants. Mariah, oblivious to the emotional turmoil swirling around her, toddled through the empty rooms, her tiny footsteps echoing in the cavernous space.

Martin watched her from the doorway, his heart heavy with a mixture of grief and guilt. He had uprooted her from her familiar surroundings, torn her away from her mother, all in the name of safety. He had made a promise to protect her, but at what cost?

He sank onto the bare mattress in the corner of the bedroom, the springs creaking under his weight. The silence of the apartment was deafening, amplifying the loneliness that gnawed at him. He had never felt so alone, so adrift.

The familiar comforts of their old home, the shared memories that clung to every corner, were now a distant echo. The laughter that had once filled their lives had been replaced by a deafening silence, a void that threatened to swallow him whole.

He reached for his phone, his fingers hovering over Rebekah's contact. A part of him longed to hear her voice, to feel the warmth of her touch, to believe that everything would be alright. But he knew that was a dangerous illusion.

He had seen the darkness in her eyes, the twisted pleasure she took in inflicting pain. He had felt the sting of her blows, the weight of her rage. He knew that returning to her would be a death sentence, a slow and agonizing descent into despair.

He put his phone down, his hand trembling. He couldn't let himself fall back into that trap. He had to focus on the present, on building a new life for himself and Mariah.

He stood up and began to unpack the few belongings they had brought with them. He arranged Mariah's toys in a neat pile on the floor, hung their clothes in the empty closet, and placed a few framed photos on the dresser.

As he worked, a sense of purpose began to fill the void within him. He was creating a home for himself and his daughter, a safe haven where they could heal and rebuild.

He made a simple meal of grilled cheese and tomato soup, Mariah's favorite. He watched as she devoured her food, her chubby cheeks smeared with orange, her eyes sparkling with delight.

After dinner, he gave her a bath, reading her a bedtime story as she soaked in the warm water. He tucked her into bed, singing her a lullaby as she drifted off to sleep.

As he sat beside her crib, watching her chest rise and fall with each gentle breath, a wave of love washed over him. This was his reason for living, the source of his strength. He would protect her, nurture her, and give her everything she needed to thrive.

He tiptoed out of the room, leaving the door cracked open. He returned to the living room, where he sank onto the couch, exhaustion finally catching up with him.

He closed his eyes, his mind racing with a whirlwind of thoughts. He had made a difficult decision, one that would have a lasting impact on his and Mariah's lives. He had chosen the unknown over the familiar, the uncertainty of the future over the comfort of the past.

But he knew it was the right decision. He had to break free from the cycle of abuse, to create a safe and healthy environment for his daughter. He had to believe that there was a brighter future waiting for them, a future filled with love, laughter, and peace.

As he drifted off to sleep, a single thought echoed in his mind: This was just the beginning. The road ahead would be long and arduous, but he was determined to walk it, one step at a time, with Mariah by his side. He would not let the darkness of the past define their future.

———

The apartment's unfamiliar silence was a stark contrast to the chaos that had erupted on Martin's phone. It buzzed incessantly, the screen flashing with Rebekah's name and a barrage of desperate messages.

"Martin, please answer. I'm so sorry."

"I didn't mean what I said. I was just upset."

"Come home. We can work this out."

"Please, Martin. Don't leave me. I need you."

Martin stared at the screen, his heart aching with a mixture of pity and anger. He knew Rebekah's pleas were not genuine. They were a desperate attempt to manipulate him, to lure him back into the toxic cycle of abuse. He had seen this pattern before, the tearful apologies followed by the inevitable return to violence.

He silenced his phone, a wave of exhaustion washing over him. He had barely slept the night before, his mind a whirlwind of anxiety and guilt. He had made the right decision, he knew that, but the weight of his choice pressed down on him like a heavy stone.

He picked up Mariah, who had woken up from her nap, her tiny arms reaching out for him. He held her close, her warmth and innocence a comforting contrast to the turmoil that raged within him.

"It's okay, sweetheart," he murmured, kissing the top of her head. "Daddy's here."

He carried her to the living room, where he settled into an armchair, Mariah nestled in his lap. He turned on the TV, hoping to distract himself from the incessant buzzing of his phone.

But even the mindless chatter of daytime television couldn't drown out the nagging voice in his head. What if Rebekah was really sorry? What if she was genuinely willing to change? Was he making a mistake by cutting her out of his and Mariah's lives?

He shook his head, trying to banish the doubts that plagued him. He had seen this act before, the tearful apologies, the promises of change. But they were always followed by more pain, more hurt. He couldn't allow himself to be fooled again.

His phone buzzed again, this time with a call from Rebekah. He hesitated, his finger hovering over the decline button. He took a deep breath and pressed it, silencing the insistent ringing.

A moment later, a text message flashed across the screen:

"If you don't answer, I'm coming over. I need to see Mariah."

Martin's heart pounded in his chest. He knew Rebekah was capable of anything, even violating the restraining order he had filed against her. He quickly texted back: *Do not come here. You will be arrested.*

The response was swift and chilling:

"You can't keep her from me, Martin. She's my daughter too."

Martin's grip on his phone tightened. He knew he had to protect Mariah, to shield her from Rebekah's volatile emotions. He called his lawyer, explaining the situation. The lawyer assured him that the restraining order was in place and that Rebekah would be arrested if she violated it.

Reassured, Martin turned his attention back to Mariah, who was now playing happily on the floor. He forced a smile, trying to project a sense of normalcy for her sake. But deep down, he knew that their lives had been irrevocably changed.

The next few days were a blur of legal consultations, court appearances, and endless phone calls with his lawyer. Rebekah continued to bombard him with messages and calls, her pleas growing increasingly desperate and threatening.

But Martin remained firm in his resolve. He had made the right decision, he knew that. He would not allow Rebekah to drag him and Mariah back into the abyss of her madness.

He started to create a new routine for himself and Mariah. They would wake up early, have breakfast together, and then head out to explore their new surroundings. They visited parks, playgrounds, and libraries, discovering the hidden gems of their new city.

Martin also began to reconnect with his friends and family. He spent long hours on the phone with his mother, sharing his fears and frustrations, seeking her wisdom and support. He met up with his colleagues from the FBI, finding solace in their camaraderie and understanding.

As the weeks passed, Martin began to feel a glimmer of hope. He was slowly but surely building a new life for himself and Mariah, a life free from fear and violence. He was rediscovering his own strength and resilience, his capacity for love and joy.

He knew that the road ahead would be long and challenging. There would be setbacks and obstacles, moments of doubt and despair. But he was determined to persevere, to create a brighter future for himself and his daughter. He would not let Rebekah's darkness extinguish his light.

_____

The first rays of morning sunlight streamed through the blinds, casting a warm glow over the sparsely furnished apartment. Martin stirred, his sleep-deprived eyes adjusting to the light. A soft cooing sound from the other room brought a smile to his face. Mariah was awake.

He rose from the makeshift bed he had created on the living room floor, his joints aching from the uncomfortable night. He walked to Mariah's room, his heart swelling with love as he watched her chubby arms flailing in the air, her bright blue eyes fixated on a mobile hanging above her crib.

"Good morning, my little sunshine," he said, picking her up and nuzzling her neck.

Mariah giggled, her tiny hands clutching at his shirt. Martin held her close, inhaling the sweet scent of baby powder and milk. In this moment, the weight of his worries lifted, replaced by a sense of pure joy and gratitude.

He knew that enrolling Mariah in daycare was a necessary step. He had to return to work to support them both, and he couldn't leave her alone in the apartment all day. But the thought of leaving her with strangers filled him with anxiety. What if she cried all day? What if she didn't eat? What if she got hurt?

He had spent hours researching daycare centers in the area, reading reviews, comparing prices, and visiting facilities. He had finally settled on a small, family-owned center called "Little Explorers," which had a reputation for providing a nurturing and stimulating environment for children.

The center was located in a quiet residential neighborhood, its bright yellow exterior a cheerful contrast to the drab buildings that surrounded it. Martin parked his car and lifted Mariah out of her car seat, his heart pounding in his chest.

They were greeted at the door by a warm and friendly woman named Mrs. Johnson, the owner of the center. She had a gentle smile and a reassuring presence that immediately put Martin at ease.

Mrs. Johnson led them on a tour of the facility, pointing out the various play areas, the cozy nap room, and the spacious outdoor playground. She introduced Martin to the other caregivers, a diverse group of women who all seemed to share a genuine love for children.

As Martin watched Mariah explore the brightly colored play area, interacting with the other children and caregivers, his anxiety began to fade. She seemed happy and content, her laughter ringing out as she chased after a ball or played with a doll.

Mrs. Johnson explained the center's philosophy, emphasizing the importance of play-based learning, social-emotional development, and fostering a love for learning. She assured Martin that Mariah would receive individual attention and care, and that he was welcome to visit or call anytime.

Martin left the center that day feeling a renewed sense of hope. He had found a place where Mariah would be safe, nurtured, and loved. He knew that he had made the right decision, a decision that would allow both him and Mariah to thrive.

In the weeks that followed, Martin watched with pride as Mariah blossomed in her new environment. She made friends, learned new skills, and developed a love for learning. He would often drop by during his lunch break, just to catch a glimpse of her playing and laughing with her new friends.

One afternoon, as he watched her build a tower out of blocks, he couldn't help but feel a surge of gratitude. He had given her a chance to thrive, to escape the darkness that had threatened to consume their lives. He had given her a safe haven, a place where she could grow and flourish.

As he left the center that day, his heart filled with a newfound sense of hope, he knew that he had made the right decision. He had chosen the path of healing, the path of hope, the path towards a brighter future for both himself and his beloved daughter.

Chapter 10: Starting Over

The sharp sting of antiseptic filled the air as Martin dabbed at the healing scratches on his face. The physical wounds were fading, but the emotional scars lingered, a constant reminder of the trauma he had endured. Each morning, he woke with a knot of anxiety in his stomach, a dull ache that threatened to consume him.

He knew he couldn't wallow in self-pity. He had a daughter to provide for, a life to rebuild. He had to find a way to move forward, to create a new normal for himself and Mariah.

With a renewed sense of purpose, he updated his resume, highlighting his years of experience in the FBI's cyber division. He reached out to his network of contacts, leveraging his expertise in cybersecurity to explore potential job opportunities.

Within a few weeks, he received an offer from a prestigious consulting firm in Phoenix. The position was a perfect fit for his skillset, offering him a chance to utilize his knowledge and experience to protect businesses from cyber threats.

The job was demanding, requiring long hours and intense focus. But Martin welcomed the challenge, immersing himself in the complex world of firewalls, encryption, and intrusion detection systems. He found solace in the technical intricacies of his work, the logical puzzles that demanded his full attention.

In the quiet solitude of his office, he could temporarily forget the pain and betrayal that had haunted him. He could focus on the task at hand, on the satisfaction of solving complex problems and protecting his clients' valuable assets.

His colleagues were a welcome distraction, their easy camaraderie and shared passion for technology providing a much-needed respite from his personal struggles. He found himself opening up to them, sharing bits and pieces of his story, finding solace in their empathy and understanding.

One evening, after a particularly long day at work, Martin found himself sitting at his desk, staring at a photo of Mariah. Her bright smile and sparkling eyes filled him with a sense of warmth and purpose. He knew that he was doing this for her, for their future together.

He picked up the phone and dialed his mother's number. "Hey, Mom," he said, his voice thick with emotion. "I just wanted to let you know that I got the job."

His mother's voice on the other end of the line was filled with pride and relief. "Oh, Martin, that's wonderful news! I'm so proud of you."

They talked for a while longer, Martin sharing his excitement about the new opportunity, his mother offering words of encouragement and support.

As he hung up the phone, Martin felt a surge of hope. He was starting over, building a new life for himself and Mariah. It wouldn't be easy, but he was determined to make it work. He had found a new purpose, a new passion, a new reason to wake up each morning.

He knew that the pain of his past would always be with him, a shadow lurking in the corners of his mind. But he would not let it define him. He would use it as fuel, a driving force to protect others, to make a difference in the world.

He would honor Rebekah's memory by living a life that she could never have imagined for him, a life filled with purpose, passion, and unwavering love for his daughter. He would show Mariah that even in the face of adversity, there is always hope, always a chance to start over and create a brighter future.

As he settled into his new job, Martin found himself working harder than ever before. He spent long hours at the office, poring over data, analyzing threats, and developing security protocols. He quickly earned the respect of his colleagues, his expertise and dedication earning him a reputation as a rising star in the cybersecurity field.

But even as he threw himself into his work, he never lost sight of his ultimate goal: to provide a stable and secure life for Mariah. He enrolled her in a new daycare, a nurturing environment where she could learn and grow. He spent his evenings reading to her, playing with her, and showering her with love and affection.

He knew that he couldn't erase the pain of the past, but he could create a new narrative, a story of resilience and hope. He would show Mariah that even in the darkest of times, there is always light, always a reason to keep going. He would be the father she deserved, the father she needed.

––––––––

The sterile, fluorescent-lit room of the community center felt a world away from the sterile confines of Martin's FBI office. Yet, in a strange way, it offered a similar sanctuary – a space where he could shed the weight of his professional facade and simply be a father, a man grappling with the messy complexities of life.

He sat on a colorful plastic chair, his arm wrapped protectively around Mariah, who clung to his side, her wide blue eyes scanning the room with a mix of curiosity and trepidation. A handful of other children, ranging in age from toddlers to preteens, milled about the room, their faces reflecting a kaleidoscope of emotions: sadness, anger, confusion, and a flicker of hope.

The support group was held in a corner of the room, a circle of chairs arranged around a low table laden with crayons, coloring books, and stuffed animals. Martin and Mariah joined the circle, their arrival met with warm smiles and welcoming nods from the other parents and children.

The facilitator, a gentle woman named Mrs. Thompson, introduced herself and explained the purpose of the group. "This is a safe space for children and parents to share their feelings about divorce," she said, her voice soft and reassuring. "It's a place to learn from each other, to find support, and to know that you're not alone."

She then invited the children to introduce themselves and share a little about their experiences. One by one, the children spoke, their voices hesitant at first, but growing stronger as they shared their stories.

A young boy named Ethan spoke of his sadness at seeing his parents argue, his confusion about why they couldn't just be friends. A girl named Lily shared her anger at her father for leaving, her fear that he didn't love her anymore.

Mariah, emboldened by the other children's openness, spoke up. "I miss my mommy," she said, her voice barely a whisper.

Martin's heart ached at her words. He knew that Mariah was struggling to understand the complexities of their situation, the reasons behind his decision to leave Rebekah.

He squeezed her hand reassuringly, his voice thick with emotion.

"I know you do, sweetheart," he said. "But Mommy is sick, and she needs help. We'll see her again soon, but for now, we need to be strong for each other."

Mariah nodded, her eyes filled with tears. Martin wiped them away with his thumb, his heart swelling with love and protectiveness for his daughter.

As the session progressed, the children began to interact with each other, their initial shyness melting away as they found common ground in their shared experiences. They drew pictures together, built towers out of blocks, and shared stories about their pets and favorite toys.

Martin watched Mariah as she played with the other children, a smile spreading across his face. He had been so worried about how she would cope with the separation, but she seemed to be thriving in this supportive environment.

Meanwhile, Martin found himself drawn into conversation with the other parents. They shared their own experiences of divorce, the challenges they had faced, the lessons they had learned. They offered each other advice, encouragement, and a shoulder to cry on.

Martin found solace in their stories, realizing that he was not alone in his struggles. He learned valuable strategies for co-parenting, for explaining the situation to Mariah in a way she could understand, and for navigating the emotional rollercoaster of divorce.

As the session came to a close, Martin felt a renewed sense of hope. He had found a community of support, a group of people who understood the unique challenges faced by single parents and children of divorce. He knew that he and Mariah would face many more challenges in the months and years to come, but he also knew that they were not alone. They had each other, and they had a growing network of friends and allies who would be there for them every step of the way.

As they left the community center, Mariah reached out and grabbed Martin's hand, her small fingers entwining with his. He looked down at her, her face radiant with a newfound sense of belonging.

"I like it here, Daddy," she said, her voice filled with excitement. "Can we come back next week?"

Martin smiled, his heart overflowing with love and gratitude. "Yes, sweetheart," he replied. "We can come back next week. And the week after that. And the week after that."

They walked hand in hand towards the car, their steps light and hopeful. The sun shone brightly overhead, a symbol of the new beginning that awaited them.

———

Months had passed since Martin left Rebekah. The legal battles raged on, but with the unwavering support of Helen, Mariah flourished under his sole custody. His new job at the cybersecurity firm provided a much-needed distraction, the complex challenges a balm for his wounded soul. Yet, the silence of his apartment in the evenings, once filled with Rebekah's laughter, now echoed with the ghosts of their shattered love.

The encouragement from his therapist and his mother led him to dip his toe into the dating pool. He joined a local hiking group, signed up for salsa lessons, and even tried his hand at online dating. He met a few interesting women, each encounter a mix of excitement and trepidation.

One such woman was Sarah, a vivacious librarian with a quick wit and a love for obscure novels. They had met at a book club meeting, their shared passion for literature sparking an instant connection. Martin found himself drawn to her warmth and intelligence, her infectious laughter a stark contrast to the tense silence he had grown accustomed to.

Their first date was at a cozy wine bar, the dim lighting and soft jazz music creating an intimate atmosphere. Sarah, her eyes sparkling with amusement, regaled him with stories of her eccentric patrons and her latest literary discoveries. Martin, in turn, shared anecdotes from his time in the FBI, carefully omitting the details of his recent trauma.

As the night progressed, Martin found himself relaxing, enjoying Sarah's company. He felt a flicker of hope, a possibility that perhaps he could find happiness again.

But as they walked back to their cars, a familiar wave of doubt washed over him. He hesitated, his hand hovering over the door handle.

"I had a really nice time," Sarah said, her smile genuine.

Martin nodded, his throat tightening. "Me too," he managed, his voice barely a whisper.

He wanted to lean in and kiss her, to prolong the fleeting sense of connection he felt with her. But a voice in his head, a dark whisper from his past, held him back.

What if she's just like Rebekah? it hissed. *What if she's manipulating you, playing with your emotions?*

He pulled back, his smile faltering. "I should probably get going," he said, his voice strained.

Sarah looked at him, a flicker of disappointment in her eyes. "Okay," she said, her voice soft. "I'll see you around?"

Martin nodded, unable to meet her gaze. He got into his car and drove away, the taste of regret bitter on his tongue. He had sabotaged yet another potential connection, his fear of getting hurt again stronger than his desire for companionship.

He replayed the evening in his mind, analyzing every word, every gesture, every fleeting expression. Had he read too much into her smile? Was he projecting his own insecurities onto her?

The next day, he called Dr. Grant, seeking her guidance. He recounted the events of the date, his voice laced with self-reproach.

"I'm terrified of getting hurt again," he admitted, his voice thick with emotion. "I can't bear the thought of going through that pain again."

Dr. Grant listened patiently, her voice soothing and reassuring.
"It's understandable that you're feeling this way, Martin," she said. "Trust is a fragile thing, especially after experiencing trauma. But it's also essential for building healthy relationships."

She paused, letting her words sink in. "You can't let your past dictate your future, Martin," she continued. "You deserve to be happy, to find love again. But in order to do that, you need to learn to trust again, to open your heart to the possibility of new connections."

Martin sighed, his shoulders slumping. "It's easier said than done," he said. "How do I know who to trust? How do I protect myself from getting hurt again?"

Dr. Grant smiled gently. "There are no guarantees in life, Martin," she said. "But you can learn to recognize the signs of healthy and unhealthy relationships. You can set boundaries, communicate your needs clearly, and listen to your instincts."

She paused, her gaze steady. "Most importantly," she said, "you need to be patient with yourself. Healing takes time, and it's okay to feel scared and vulnerable. But don't let fear hold you back from finding happiness."

Martin thanked her for her words of wisdom, a renewed sense of determination filling him. He knew that he had a long road ahead of him, but he was willing to face it, one step at a time. He would not let the ghosts of his past haunt his present or rob him of his future.

He would learn to trust again, to open his heart to the possibility of love. He would find a way to balance his desire for companionship with his fear of getting hurt again. He would create a new life for himself and Mariah, a life filled with love, laughter, and the joy of shared experiences. He would not let the darkness win.

Chapter 11: Legal Battles

The conference room was cold and impersonal, the sterile white walls amplifying the tension that crackled in the air. Martin sat at one end of the long, mahogany table, his lawyer, a steely-eyed woman named Ms. Roberts, at his side. Rebekah sat opposite him, flanked by her attorney, a slick, silver-haired man named Mr. Anderson.

Their eyes met for a fleeting moment, a silent exchange of animosity and hurt. Martin's gaze was resolute, hardened by months of emotional turmoil and legal battles. Rebekah's eyes, once filled with warmth and affection, now burned with a cold fury.

"Let's begin," Ms. Roberts said, her voice brisk and businesslike. "As you know, we're here to discuss the terms of your divorce."

She laid out a stack of documents on the table, each page representing another battleground in their war of attrition. Custody arrangements, financial settlements, division of assets – every aspect of their shared life now subject to legal scrutiny and dissection.

Mr. Anderson cleared his throat, his voice smooth and condescending. "My client is prepared to be reasonable," he said, his eyes fixed on Martin. "But she will not be taken advantage of."

Martin bristled at the insinuation. He had never taken advantage of Rebekah, had always put her needs before his own. But now, she was twisting the narrative, painting him as the villain in their shared tragedy.

"Reasonable?" he scoffed, his voice laced with bitterness. "You call it reasonable to demand sole custody of Mariah after everything you've done?"

Rebekah flinched, her eyes narrowing. "I'm her mother," she hissed. "I have a right to be in her life."

"You forfeited that right when you pulled a knife on me in front of her," Martin retorted, his voice rising. "You put her in danger, Rebekah. You terrorized her."

Rebekah's face contorted with rage. "Don't you dare try to turn my daughter against me!" she shouted, her voice echoing through the room. "She needs me, Martin. She needs her mother."

Ms. Roberts intervened, her voice calm but firm. "Let's try to keep things civil, shall we? We're here to find a solution that's in the best interests of the child."

She turned to Mr. Anderson. "I understand your client's desire for custody," she said, "but given the circumstances, we believe that sole custody with supervised visitation rights for your client is the most appropriate arrangement."

Mr. Anderson leaned back in his chair, a smug smile playing on his lips. "I'm afraid my client disagrees," he said. "She believes that joint custody is the only fair solution."

Martin's blood ran cold. He couldn't imagine leaving Mariah alone with Rebekah, not after everything that had happened. The thought of his daughter being exposed to her mother's volatile moods and unpredictable behavior filled him with dread.

"Joint custody is out of the question," he said, his voice firm. "Rebekah is not stable. She's a danger to herself and to others."

Rebekah let out a derisive laugh. "Oh, please," she sneered. "You're just trying to punish me. You're using Mariah as a pawn in your little revenge game."

Martin's fists clenched, his anger threatening to boil over. He wanted to reach across the table and shake her, to make her see the damage she had caused. But he knew that would only play into her hands.

Ms. Roberts stepped in again, her voice soothing but authoritative. "Let's not get sidetracked by personal accusations," she said. "We're here to discuss the facts, not to rehash old arguments."

She turned to Mr. Anderson. "We have ample evidence of your client's abusive behavior," she said, her voice cold and precise. "Medical records, police reports, witness statements. We believe that it's in Mariah's best interests to remain in her father's care, with supervised visitation for your client."

Mr. Anderson shrugged, his demeanor nonchalant. "We'll see what the judge has to say about that," he said, a smug smile returning to his lips.

The negotiations continued for hours, each side entrenched in their positions, unwilling to budge. Martin felt exhausted, drained by the emotional toll of the proceedings. He just wanted it to be over, to have a resolution so he could move on with his life and focus on healing.

But he also knew that he couldn't give up, couldn't compromise on Mariah's safety. He had to fight, to protect her from the woman who had once been his everything.

As the meeting drew to a close, no agreement had been reached. Both sides agreed to reconvene the following week, armed with additional evidence and arguments to support their respective positions.

Martin left the courthouse feeling emotionally exhausted but determined. He knew that the battle was far from over, but he was ready to fight, to do whatever it took to protect his daughter. He would not rest until Mariah was safe, until he had created a new life for them, a life free from fear and filled with love.

———

The imposing grandeur of the Maricopa County Superior Court building loomed over Martin as he walked up the steps, his hand tightly gripping Mariah's. The little girl, dressed in her favorite pink sundress, looked up at him with wide, curious eyes, oblivious to the gravity of the situation. Martin offered her a reassuring smile, his heart heavy with the weight of the impending legal battle.

The courtroom was packed, the air thick with tension. Martin and his attorney, Ms. Roberts, sat on one side of the aisle, their faces grim and determined. Rebekah and her lawyer, Mr. Anderson, occupied the other side, their expressions a mix of defiance and feigned innocence.

As the judge entered the courtroom, a hush fell over the crowd. Martin's heart pounded in his chest, his palms sweaty. He had prepared for this day, meticulously documenting every instance of abuse, every threatening message, every outburst of rage. Yet, as he glanced at Rebekah, a flicker of doubt crept into his mind. Could he really do this? Could he publicly expose the woman he had once loved, the mother of his child, as the monster she had become?

The judge called the case, and the proceedings began. Mr. Anderson, his voice dripping with practiced eloquence, painted a picture of Rebekah as a loving mother who had been unfairly maligned by her estranged husband. He argued that Martin was exaggerating her flaws, manipulating the facts to gain an advantage in the custody battle.

"My client is a devoted mother who has always put her child's needs first," he declared, his voice booming through the courtroom. "She has made mistakes, yes, but she is deeply remorseful and committed to making amends."

He paused, his eyes scanning the jury, his voice lowering to a conspiratorial whisper. "I ask you to consider the possibility that Mr. Reed is not the innocent victim he portrays himself to be.

Perhaps he is simply trying to punish my client for daring to challenge his authority, to break free from his control."

Martin listened with mounting anger, his hands clenching into fists. He wanted to jump up and shout the truth, to expose Rebekah's lies and manipulations. But he knew that he had to remain calm, to trust in his lawyer, to let the evidence speak for itself.

Ms. Roberts, her voice sharp and incisive, countered Mr. Anderson's arguments with a barrage of irrefutable facts. She presented the medical records documenting Martin's injuries, the police reports detailing Rebekah's violent outbursts, and the testimonies of witnesses who had witnessed her erratic behavior firsthand.

"My client has been subjected to a campaign of terror," she declared, her voice ringing with righteous indignation. "He has been physically assaulted, emotionally manipulated, and psychologically abused. He has lived in constant fear for his safety and the safety of his daughter."

She paused, her gaze fixed on the judge. "We are not here to punish Mrs. Reed," she continued. "We are here to protect Mariah. She deserves to grow up in a safe and stable environment, free from the trauma and instability that her mother has inflicted upon her."

Martin listened with a mix of pride and sorrow. He was grateful for Ms. Roberts' unwavering support, her fierce determination to advocate for him and Mariah. But he also couldn't shake the sadness that gnawed at him, the realization that his marriage had crumbled into such a bitter and public spectacle.

The hearing lasted for hours, each side presenting their evidence and arguments, the tension in the courtroom building with each passing minute. Martin's nerves were frayed, his body exhausted from the emotional strain. But he held on to the image of Mariah's smiling face, the knowledge that he was fighting for her future.

Finally, the judge called for a recess. Martin and Ms. Roberts retreated to a small conference room, their faces etched with worry.

"How do you think it's going?" Martin asked, his voice barely a whisper.

Ms. Roberts offered him a reassuring smile. "We've presented a strong case, Martin," she said. "But ultimately, the decision rests with the judge. We just have to trust in the process."

Martin nodded, his heart heavy with uncertainty. He knew that the outcome of this hearing would determine the course of his and Mariah's lives. He could only hope that justice would prevail, that the truth would be revealed, and that Mariah would be protected from the darkness that had threatened to consume their family.

———

The courtroom buzzed with hushed whispers and the rustling of papers as Judge Morrison, a stern-faced woman with a reputation for fairness, prepared to deliver her verdict. Martin's heart pounded in his chest, a drumbeat of anxiety and anticipation. Beside him, Ms. Roberts, his lawyer, squeezed his hand reassuringly, her eyes conveying a quiet confidence that belied the tension of the moment.

Across the aisle, Rebekah sat ramrod straight, her face a mask of stoicism. Martin couldn't read her thoughts, but the rigid set of her jaw and the flicker of defiance in her eyes betrayed the turmoil raging within her.

"In the matter of Reed v. Reed," Judge Morrison began, her voice echoing through the hushed courtroom, "this court has carefully considered the evidence presented by both parties, including testimony, medical records, and police reports."

Martin held his breath, his gaze fixed on the judge's face, searching for any clue to her decision. Beside him, Mariah squirmed restlessly in her booster seat, her attention captured by the colorful mural on the back wall of the courtroom.

"It is clear," Judge Morrison continued, "that this has been a difficult and emotionally charged case. Both parties have experienced significant pain and suffering. However, the primary concern of this court is the well-being of the child, Mariah Reed."

Martin's grip tightened on Mariah's hand, a surge of protectiveness washing over him.

"Based on the evidence presented," Judge Morrison continued, "this court finds that the mother, Rebekah Reed, has engaged in a pattern of abusive behavior towards her husband, Martin Reed. This behavior includes emotional manipulation, verbal abuse, and physical violence."

A gasp escaped Rebekah's lips, her face flushing with anger. Her attorney, Mr. Anderson, placed a restraining hand on her arm, his expression warning her to remain silent.

"Furthermore," Judge Morrison continued, "this court finds that Mrs. Reed's mental instability poses a significant risk to the safety and well-being of the child. Therefore, this court awards sole legal and physical custody of Mariah Reed to her father, Martin Reed."

A wave of relief washed over Martin, his shoulders sagging as the tension drained from his body. He glanced at Ms.

Roberts, who offered him a triumphant smile. Beside him, Mariah, oblivious to the significance of the moment, continued to gaze at the mural, her face a picture of innocence.

"Mrs. Reed," Judge Morrison continued, her voice hardening, "you will be granted supervised visitation rights with the child, pending a psychological evaluation and completion of an anger management program. Failure to comply with these conditions will result in the termination of your visitation rights."

Rebekah's composure finally cracked. She jumped to her feet, her voice shrill with outrage. "This is an injustice!" she screamed. "You can't take my child away from me! I'm her mother!"

Mr. Anderson quickly rose, his hand firmly on her arm, trying to restrain her. "Mrs. Reed, please," he said, his voice low and urgent. "Control yourself."

But Rebekah was beyond reason. She wrenched her arm free from his grasp and lunged towards Martin, her face contorted with rage.

"You'll never get away with this!" she screamed. "I'll fight you tooth and nail. You'll never take my daughter from me!"

Court security officers quickly intervened, restraining Rebekah and escorting her out of the courtroom. Her screams echoed down the hallway, a chilling reminder of the danger she posed.

Martin sat in stunned silence, his mind reeling from the emotional rollercoaster of the past few hours. He had won, he had been granted sole custody of Mariah. But there was no sense of victory, only a profound sadness and a lingering fear for the future.

He knew that this was not the end of the battle. Rebekah would not give up easily. She would fight him every step of the way, using every weapon in her arsenal to try and regain control of her daughter. He would have to remain vigilant, protect Mariah at all costs, and prepare for the long and arduous road ahead.

But in this moment, as he held his daughter close, he felt a glimmer of hope. He had taken the first step towards a brighter future, a future where Mariah would be safe, loved, and protected from the darkness that had threatened to consume their lives.

Chapter 12: Healing and Reflection

The familiar scent of lavender incense and the muted hum of the air conditioner greeted Martin as he entered Dr. Grant's office. He sank into the well-worn armchair, a wave of exhaustion washing over him. The legal battles had taken their toll, leaving him physically and emotionally drained. Yet, amidst the exhaustion, he felt a glimmer of hope. The court's decision had granted him sole custody of Mariah, a victory that had come at a great cost, but a victory nonetheless.

Dr. Grant sat opposite him, her warm smile offering a welcome respite from the harsh realities of his life. "Welcome back, Martin," she said, her voice soft and reassuring. "How are you feeling?"

Martin hesitated, his fingers tracing the worn leather armrests of the chair. "Relieved," he admitted. "But also… empty."

He paused, his gaze drifting to the abstract painting on the wall. "I won," he continued, his voice barely a whisper. "But it doesn't feel like a victory. It feels like… loss."

Dr. Grant nodded, her eyes filled with understanding. "It's natural to feel conflicting emotions," she said. "You've been through a traumatic experience, and it will take time to heal. But I'm proud of you for taking the steps to protect yourself and Mariah. That takes incredible courage and strength."

Martin's eyes met hers, a flicker of gratitude in their depths. "Thank you," he said. "I couldn't have done it without your support."

Dr. Grant smiled. "You've done the hard work, Martin," she said. "I'm just here to guide you through the healing process."

She paused, her gaze thoughtful. "Now that the legal battles are mostly behind you, it's time to focus on your own healing," she said. "We need to explore the root causes of your attraction to Rebekah, the patterns that led you to this point."

Martin shifted in his chair, a sense of unease settling over him. He had never delved into his past relationships before, never questioned his choices in partners. But he knew that in order to heal, he had to confront the demons that lurked in the shadows of his subconscious.

He began to speak, hesitantly at first, then with growing confidence as the words poured out of him. He spoke of his childhood, of growing up with a distant father and a codependent mother. He described his need for validation, his attraction to strong, independent women who reminded him of his mother.

He talked about Rebekah, about the initial spark of attraction, the intoxicating whirlwind of their early romance. He spoke of her passion, her intelligence, her undeniable charisma. But he also acknowledged the red flags he had ignored, the subtle signs of instability that he had dismissed as quirks or eccentricities.

As he spoke, he began to see patterns emerge, patterns of behavior that he had unknowingl repeated in his past relationships. He saw how his need for validation had led him to women who were emotionally unavailable, women who mirrored the dysfunctional dynamics of his childhood.

Dr. Grant listened intently, her pen occasionally scribbling on her notepad. She gently guided the conversation, asking probing questions, helping Martin to connect the dots between his past and his present.

"It's not your fault, Martin," she said, her voice filled with compassion. "You were drawn to Rebekah because she triggered familiar patterns, patterns that were ingrained in you from childhood. But you can break those patterns. You can learn to set healthy boundaries, to recognize red flags, and to choose partners who are capable of reciprocating your love and respect."

Martin nodded, his mind reeling from the revelations. He had never thought of himself as a victim, but he realized now that he had been trapped in a cycle of unhealthy relationships, drawn to women who were emotionally unavailable or abusive.

He made a vow to himself that day, a promise to break free from the past and create a healthier future. He would work on his own healing, learn to love and respect himself, and choose partners who would do the same.

He left Dr. Grant's office that day feeling both exhausted and empowered. He knew that the road to recovery would be long and arduous, but he was determined to walk it. He would not let the trauma of his past define him. He would rise above it, stronger and wiser, ready to embrace a future filled with love, joy, and healthy relationships.

———

The worn leather journal felt comforting in Martin's hands, its blank pages a silent invitation to spill his soul's ink. He sat at his makeshift desk in the corner of the living room, the only sound the rhythmic ticking of the wall clock and Mariah's soft breathing from the bedroom. The weight of the day – the endless paperwork at work, the strained phone calls with his lawyer, the worry gnawing at the edges of his mind – seemed to lift as he picked up his pen.

Day 1, he wrote, the date scrawled in bold letters at the top of the page.

I never thought I'd be writing in a journal, he mused, a wry smile tugging at his lips. *But then again, I never thought I'd be divorced, a single father, rebuilding my life from scratch.*

He paused, his pen hovering over the page. Where to begin? The story of his broken marriage was a tangled web of love, betrayal, and deceit. He could start with the day he met Rebekah, the spark of attraction that had ignited like a wildfire, consuming them both in its intensity. He could write about the early days of their relationship, the laughter, the shared dreams, the whispered promises of forever.

But he decided to start with the ending, with the shattered remnants of their love. He wrote about the pain, the fear, the helplessness he had felt as he endured Rebekah's escalating abuse. He described the moment he realized he had to leave, the agonizing decision to protect himself and his daughter from further harm.

I never thought I could love someone so much, and yet be so terrified of them at the same time, he wrote, the words flowing onto the page in a torrent of raw emotion. *I feel like a part of me has died, a part of me that believed in love, in the possibility of happily ever after.*

He paused, his hand cramping from the intensity of his grip on the pen. He took a deep breath, trying to steady his trembling hand.

But I also feel a strange sense of liberation, he continued. *A weight has been lifted from my shoulders, a darkness dispelled. I am no longer a prisoner in my own home, a victim of someone else's demons.*

He wrote about the challenges of being a single parent, the sleepless nights, the endless worries, the constant juggling of work and childcare. But he also wrote about the joy he found in Mariah's smile, the warmth of her hugs, the unconditional love that radiated from her tiny being.

She is my reason for living, he wrote, a tear rolling down his cheek.
She is my hope, my inspiration, my everything.
He continued to write, filling page after page with his thoughts and feelings. He wrote about the anger he felt towards Rebekah, the betrayal that had shattered his trust. He wrote about the guilt he felt for not seeing the warning signs sooner, for not protecting himself and his daughter from harm.

But he also wrote about the lessons he had learned, the hard-won wisdom that had emerged from the ashes of his broken marriage. He had learned that love is not enough, that trust and respect are the cornerstones of any healthy relationship. He had learned that he was stronger than he ever thought possible, that he could overcome even the most devastating of challenges.

He had learned that even in the darkest of times, there is always a glimmer of hope, a chance for redemption and renewal.

As he closed his journal, a sense of peace washed over him. He had given voice to his pain, his anger, his fears. He had acknowledged the darkness, but he had also found the light.

He knew that the road to healing would be long and arduous, but he was determined to walk it. He would not let the trauma of his past define him. He would use it as fuel, a catalyst for growth and transformation.

He would emerge from this ordeal a stronger, wiser, and more compassionate man. He would be a role model for his daughter, showing her that even in the face of adversity, it is possible to find hope, to find love, to find happiness.

He would not let the darkness win.

———

The familiar smell of beeswax and old wood filled Martin's nostrils as he stepped into the small, dimly lit chapel. Dust motes danced in the sunlight streaming through the stained glass windows, casting a kaleidoscope of colors across the worn wooden pews. The chapel had been a sanctuary for him as a child, a place of solace and peace where he had sought refuge from the turmoil of his home life.

He walked down the aisle, his footsteps echoing in the empty space. He knelt at the altar, his head bowed, his hands clasped in prayer. The familiar words of the Lord's Prayer came to him unbidden, a childhood memory surfacing from the depths of his subconscious.

"Our Father, who art in heaven, hallowed be Thy name…"

He whispered the words, his voice trembling at first, then growing stronger as he poured out his heart to a God he had long neglected. He confessed his sins, his anger, his resentment towards Rebekah. He begged for forgiveness, for guidance, for the strength to move forward.

As he prayed, a sense of peace began to wash over him, a warmth spreading through his chest. It was as if a weight had been lifted from his shoulders, a burden he had been carrying for far too long.

He rose from his knees, feeling a newfound sense of purpose and clarity. He lit a candle, its flickering flame a symbol of hope in the darkness that had enveloped him. He sat down in a pew, closing his eyes, his mind open to the divine.

He began to meditate, focusing on his breath, letting go of the thoughts and emotions that cluttered his mind. He envisioned himself surrounded by a white light, a protective shield against the negativity that had poisoned his life. He repeated a simple mantra, "I am strong. I am worthy. I am loved."

As he meditated, he felt a profound sense of peace and connectedness. He realized that he was not alone in his struggles, that there was a higher power guiding and protecting him. He felt a renewed sense of faith, a belief that he could overcome any obstacle, any adversity, with God's help.

He continued to attend church regularly, finding solace in the rituals and traditions of his childhood faith. He joined a men's Bible study group, where he shared his experiences and found support from other men who had faced similar challenges. He volunteered at the church's soup kitchen, serving meals to the homeless and less fortunate, finding purpose in helping others.

He also began to practice meditation and mindfulness in his daily life. He would take a few minutes each day to sit in silence, focusing on his breath, grounding himself in the present moment. He found that these practices helped him to manage his anxiety, to stay calm and centered even in the face of stress and adversity.

As he deepened his spiritual practice, he began to see the world in a new light. He realized that his experiences, both the good and the bad, had shaped him into the man he was today. He had learned valuable   lessons about love, loss,   forgiveness,   and resilience.

He began to see his failed marriage not as a failure, but as a learning experience, a necessary step on his journey towards wholeness. He realized that he had been holding onto anger and resentment towards Rebekah, emotions that were only poisoning his own soul.

He made a conscious decision to forgive her, not for her sake, but for his own. He recognized that forgiveness didn't mean condoning her actions, but rather, releasing himself from the burden of anger and bitterness.

As he let go of the past, he felt a weight lifted from his heart. He was no longer defined by the trauma he had endured, but by the strength and resilience he had found within himself.

He had reconnected with his faith, not as a crutch, but as a source of strength and guidance. He had learned to find solace in prayer and meditation, to draw on the wisdom of his spiritual tradition.

And as he moved forward on his journey of healing, he knew that he was not alone. He had the love and support of his family and friends, the guidance of his therapist, and the unwavering presence of a higher power to guide him through the darkness and into the light.

Chapter 13: A New Beginning

The moving van's engine rumbled to a stop, its metallic groan echoing in the quiet suburban street. Martin emerged from the driver's seat, stretching his stiff muscles as he surveyed their new home. It wasn't a grand mansion or a sprawling estate, but a modest single-story house with a welcoming porch and a sprawling backyard. Its faded yellow paint and overgrown flower beds hinted at neglect, but Martin saw potential, a blank canvas upon which he and Mariah could paint a new life.

Mariah, clutching her favorite stuffed unicorn, peeked out from behind Martin's legs, her eyes wide with a mix of excitement and apprehension. "Is this our new home, Daddy?" she asked, her voice barely a whisper.

Martin knelt down, his eyes meeting hers. "It is, sweetheart," he said, a warm smile spreading across his face. "And it's going to be amazing."

He held out his hand, and Mariah eagerly took it, her small fingers intertwining with his. Together, they walked up the creaky wooden steps to the front door, a sense of anticipation building within them.

As they entered the house, a musty smell of disuse greeted them. The rooms were empty, their bare walls echoing with the silence of neglect. But Martin saw past the dust and cobwebs, envisioning a home filled with laughter, love, and the warmth of family.

"What do you think, Mariah?" he asked, his voice filled with excitement. "Do you like it?"

Mariah looked around, her eyes wide with wonder. "It's big!" she exclaimed, her voice filled with awe.

"It is," Martin agreed. "And it's all ours."

They spent the rest of the day exploring the house, their imaginations running wild as they envisioned each room transformed. Mariah claimed the bedroom with the bay window as her own, declaring that it would be her "princess castle." Martin smiled, envisioning the room filled with colorful murals and overflowing with toys.

The following day, the moving van arrived, its contents disgorged into the living room. Martin and Mariah surveyed the jumble of boxes and furniture, their excitement growing with each unpacked item.

Mariah squealed with delight as she discovered her old rocking horse, its worn paint a testament to countless hours of play. She immediately climbed aboard, rocking back and forth with glee.

Martin smiled, his heart swelling with love for his daughter. He was determined to create a happy and stable home for her, a place where she could feel safe and loved.

They spent the next few weeks decorating, transforming the once-drab house into a cozy haven. They painted the walls in bright, cheerful colors, hung artwork that Mariah had created at daycare, and filled the shelves with books and toys.

The kitchen became the heart of their home, a place where they cooked together, shared meals, and laughed until their sides ached. The living room was transformed into a cozy den, with plush pillows and blankets scattered on the floor, perfect for snuggling up with a good book or watching movies together.

Mariah's bedroom was a magical wonderland, adorned with fairy lights, butterfly decals, and a canopy bed draped in sheer pink fabric. It was a space where she could let her imagination run wild, a place where she could dream big and believe in the impossible.

As the weeks turned into months, the house began to feel like a home. It was a place where they felt safe, loved, and truly happy. The echoes of the past faded away, replaced by the joyful sounds of laughter, music, and the patter of tiny feet.

One evening, as they sat on the porch swing, watching the sunset paint the sky in hues of orange and pink, Martin looked at Mariah, her face glowing with contentment.

"Do you like our new home, sweetheart?" he asked, his voice filled with love.

Mariah nodded, her smile wide and bright. "I love it, Daddy," she said, snuggling closer to him. "It's the best home ever."

Martin's heart swelled with joy. He had given Mariah a fresh start, a chance to heal and thrive. He had created a home filled with love and laughter, a sanctuary from the storms of the past.

As he held his daughter close, he knew that he had made the right decision. He had chosen the path of hope, the path of healing, the path towards a brighter future for both himself and his beloved daughter.

———

The air hung heavy with a mixture of antiseptic and stale coffee in the cramped meeting room of the "New Horizons" domestic violence shelter. Martin sat in a circle of mismatched chairs, surrounded by a diverse group of men, their faces etched with the scars of physical and emotional trauma.

He fidgeted with the frayed collar of his shirt, his nerves tingling with a mix of anticipation and apprehension. This was his first time volunteering at the shelter, a decision he had made after weeks of soul-searching and encouragement from his therapist. He had spent countless hours researching the issue of domestic violence, reading harrowing accounts of survivors, and learning about the resources available to victims.

The group leader, a tall, imposing man with a gentle voice and kind eyes, began the meeting with a brief meditation exercise. As Martin closed his eyes, focusing on his breath, he could feel the tension slowly draining from his body. The weight of his own experiences, the memories of Rebekah's abuse, seemed to lighten as he connected with the collective energy of the room.

After the meditation, the group leader invited everyone to share their stories. One by one, the men spoke, their voices hesitant at first, but growing stronger as they shared their experiences. They spoke of the betrayal, the fear, the shame, the isolation. They spoke of the courage it took to leave, the strength it took to rebuild their lives.

Martin listened intently, his heart aching with each story. He heard echoes of his own pain in their words, the same sense of isolation and despair that had once consumed him. But he also heard hope, resilience, and the unwavering determination to overcome adversity.

When it was his turn to speak, he took a deep breath, his voice trembling slightly. "My name is Martin," he began. "I'm a survivor of domestic violence."

The room fell silent, every eye fixed on him. He continued, his voice growing stronger as he shared his story. He spoke of his whirlwind romance with Rebekah, their shared dreams and aspirations, the insidious creep of emotional abuse, and the terrifying escalation to physical violence.

He recounted the night Rebekah pulled a knife on him in front of their daughter, the chilling realization that he was no longer safe in his own home. He described the agonizing decision to leave, the legal battles, the sleepless nights filled with worry and self-doubt.

But he also spoke of the strength he found in his daughter, the unwavering support of his mother-in-law, and the transformative power of therapy. He shared how he had learned to forgive himself for his past mistakes, to set healthy boundaries, and to believe in the possibility of a brighter future.

As he spoke, a sense of camaraderie filled the room. The other men nodded in agreement, their faces reflecting a shared understanding of the pain and triumph he described. They offered words of encouragement, their voices filled with empathy and respect.

When Martin finished his story, a heavy silence hung in the air. Then, one of the men, a burly biker named Jake, spoke up. "Thank you for sharing, Martin," he said, his voice gruff but sincere. "Your story is powerful. It gives me hope."

Other men echoed his sentiments, their words a chorus of solidarity and support. Martin felt a warmth spread through him, a sense of belonging he had not felt in a long time.

In the weeks that followed, Martin became a regular at the shelter. He facilitated group sessions, listened to other survivors' stories, and offered his own experiences as a source of hope and inspiration. He helped men develop safety plans, connected them with legal resources, and provided a listening ear and a shoulder to lean on.

He found a sense of purpose in his volunteer work, a way to channel his pain into something positive. He realized that by sharing his story, he was not only helping others but also healing himself. The act of speaking his truth, of connecting with others who understood his pain, was a cathartic experience that allowed him to release the burden of shame and guilt that had haunted him for so long.

One evening, as he was leaving the shelter, a young man named Carlos approached him. "Martin," he said, his voice hesitant, "I just wanted to thank you. Your story gave me the courage to leave my abusive partner. You showed me that there is hope, that there is a life after abuse."

Martin smiled, his heart swelling with pride and gratitude. "You're welcome, Carlos," he said. "Remember, you're not alone. There are people who care, people who want to help. And you're stronger than you think."

As Martin walked away from the shelter that night, the weight on his shoulders felt a little lighter. He had found a new purpose, a new meaning in his life. He was no longer a victim, but a survivor, a beacon of hope for others who were struggling to break free from the cycle of abuse.

The bookstore was a haven of tranquility, its shelves overflowing with the promise of adventure, romance, and wisdom. Martin browsed the aisles, his fingers trailing along the spines of worn paperbacks and glossy hardcovers. He inhaled the comforting scent of old books, a nostalgic reminder of simpler times, a life before the storm of his marriage to Rebekah.

As he rounded a corner, he bumped into a woman clutching a stack of books, sending them tumbling to the floor. "Oh, I'm so sorry," he said, bending down to help her gather the scattered volumes.

"No worries," the woman replied, a melodious laugh escaping her lips. "I'm always a bit clumsy around books. I get lost in their worlds."

Martin looked up, his eyes meeting hers. They were a warm hazel, framed by a cascade of auburn curls. Her smile was genuine, her eyes filled with a kindness that instantly put him at ease.

"I'm Martin," he introduced himself, extending a hand.

"Sarah," she replied, her handshake firm and confident.

They chatted as they picked up the books, discussing their favorite authors and genres. Martin learned that Sarah was a librarian at the local library, her passion for literature evident in the way her eyes lit up when she spoke about books.

"I'm actually here to pick up some new releases for the library," Sarah explained. "We're always trying to keep our collection fresh and exciting."

"I can imagine," Martin replied. "I love libraries. They're like a treasure trove of knowledge and stories."

As they talked, Martin found himself drawn to Sarah's warmth and intelligence. She was easy to talk to, her conversation flowing effortlessly from one topic to the next. He felt a spark of connection, a flicker of hope that perhaps he could find happiness again.

They exchanged numbers, promising to meet up for coffee the following week. Martin left the bookstore that day with a lighter heart, a sense of anticipation bubbling within him.

Their first coffee date turned into a long and leisurely lunch, their conversation ranging from literature to current events, from childhood dreams to adult realities. Martin shared his experience as a therapist, his passion for helping others heal from trauma. Sarah, in turn, opened up about her love for books, her dedication to her community, and her dreams of starting a literacy program for underprivileged children.

As they talked, Martin found himself drawn to Sarah's compassion and her unwavering belief in the goodness of humanity. She listened to his stories with empathy and understanding, never judging, never prying.

They began to see each other regularly, their dates a mix of casual outings and shared interests. They hiked through the scenic trails of the McDowell Sonoran Preserve, attended art exhibits at the Phoenix Art Museum, and volunteered together at a local soup kitchen.

With each encounter, Martin's trust in Sarah grew. She was patient, kind, and genuinely interested in him. She didn't push him to talk about his past, but she was always there to listen when he was ready to share.

One evening, as they sat on a bench overlooking the city lights,
Martin finally opened up about his traumatic experience with Rebekah. He spoke of the abuse, the fear, the betrayal, and the long road to recovery.

Sarah listened intently, her hand gently squeezing his. She didn't offer platitudes or false reassurances. She simply listened, her presence a silent testament to her compassion and understanding.

"I'm so sorry you went through that, Martin," she said, her voice soft and sincere. "You're so strong for getting through it."

Her words, spoken with such genuine empathy, were a balm to Martin's wounded soul. He felt seen, heard, and understood in a way he hadn't felt in a long time.

In the weeks that followed, Martin and Sarah's relationship deepened. They shared laughter, tears, and intimate moments. They supported each other through the challenges of their individual lives, celebrating each other's triumphs and offering comfort in times of need.

Martin found himself falling in love with Sarah, slowly and cautiously, building a foundation of trust and mutual respect. He learned to let go of the fear that had held him back, to embrace the vulnerability that comes with opening your heart to another.

He knew that their relationship was still in its early stages, that there were many challenges ahead. But for the first time in a long time, he felt hopeful, optimistic about the future. He had found a woman who saw him for who he truly was, a woman who loved him unconditionally, a woman who would stand by his side through thick and thin.

Chapter 14: Escalating Danger

The shrill ring of Martin's phone sliced through the calm of his office. He glanced at the caller ID – Little Explorers Daycare – and a knot of anxiety tightened in his stomach. He answered, his voice tight with apprehension.

"Hello?"

"Mr. Reed? This is Mrs. Johnson from Little Explorers. I'm calling about Mariah."

Martin's heart pounded in his chest. "Is she okay?" he asked, his voice rising an octave.

"She's fine, Mr. Reed," Mrs. Johnson reassured him. "But there's a situation... a woman is here claiming to be her mother."

Martin's blood ran cold. "Rebekah?" he asked, dread filling his voice.

"Yes," Mrs. Johnson confirmed. "She's demanding to see Mariah. We've explained that she's not allowed on the premises, but she's refusing to leave."

Martin's mind raced. Rebekah was violating the restraining order. He had to act quickly, to protect Mariah from her mother's volatile behavior.

"Mrs. Johnson, please keep Mariah safe," he said, his voice urgent.

"I'm calling the police."

He hung up and immediately dialed 911. He explained the situation to the dispatcher, his voice trembling with barely contained rage. He gave them the address of the daycare and pleaded with them to hurry.

As he waited for the police to arrive, he paced his office, his mind a whirlwind of fear and anger. How dare Rebekah violate the restraining order? How dare she put Mariah in danger?

He couldn't believe that she would stoop so low, that she would risk arrest just to see her daughter. It was a clear sign of her instability, her utter disregard for the law and for Martin's well-being.

The minutes ticked by agonizingly slowly. Martin's colleagues, sensing his distress, offered words of comfort and support, but their words fell on deaf ears. All he could think about was Mariah, her innocent face, her infectious laughter. He couldn't bear the thought of her being exposed to Rebekah's toxic presence.

Finally, the sound of sirens broke the tense silence. Martin rushed out of the office, his heart pounding in his chest. He saw two police cars pull up in front of the daycare, their lights flashing, their sirens wailing.

He ran towards the entrance, his eyes scanning the crowd of onlookers. He saw Rebekah standing by the door, her face pale and drawn, her eyes wild with desperation. Two police officers stood on either side of her, their hands resting on her arms.

As Martin approached, Rebekah's eyes locked with his, a flicker of defiance in their depths. "You can't keep her from me, Martin," she hissed. "She's my daughter."

Martin ignored her, his gaze fixed on the police officers. "She's violated the restraining order," he said, his voice firm. "She's not allowed to be here."

One of the officers nodded. "We're aware of the situation, Mr. Reed," he said. "We'll take care of this."

The officers led Rebekah away, her protests growing louder as they reached the patrol car. Martin watched as they placed her in the backseat, her face contorted with rage and frustration.

He turned and entered the daycare, his heart heavy with a mixture of relief and sadness. He found Mariah in the playroom, her face buried in Mrs. Johnson's shoulder. She looked up as he entered, her eyes wide with fear.

Martin rushed to her, scooping her up in his arms. "It's okay, sweetheart," he said, his voice thick with emotion. "Daddy's here."

He held her close, rocking her gently as she clung to him. He knew that this incident would leave a lasting scar on her young psyche, but he was determined to protect her, to shield her from the darkness that had threatened to consume their lives.

As he carried Mariah out of the daycare, he glanced back at the police car, where Rebekah sat, her face pressed against the window, her eyes filled with a venomous hatred. Martin felt a chill run down his spine, a chilling reminder of the danger they had escaped.

He knew that this was not the end, that Rebekah would continue to fight for access to Mariah. But he was prepared to face any challenge, any obstacle, to ensure his daughter's safety and well-being. He would not let Rebekah's madness poison Mariah's life. He would protect her, no matter the cost.

––––––

The days following Rebekah's arrest were a tense waiting game. Martin knew she wouldn't go down without a fight. He'd taken every precaution, changing locks, installing a security system, and keeping Mariah close at all times. But a gnawing unease lingered, a constant reminder of the storm brewing just beyond their newfound peace.

One morning, Martin woke to the insistent buzzing of his phone. He squinted at the screen, his heart sinking at the sight of

Rebekah's name. He hesitated, his finger hovering over the 'decline' button. But a morbid curiosity, a need to know what fresh torment she had concocted, made him swipe to answer.

"You can't hide from me, Martin," her voice rasped through the speaker, raw with rage. "You'll never take my daughter away from me."

Martin's grip tightened on the phone. "Rebekah, you're violating the restraining order. Stop calling me."

"A piece of paper won't stop me," she sneered. "You'll see. I'll get her back. You'll both pay for this."

The line went dead, leaving Martin with a sickening chill in the pit of his stomach. He immediately called his lawyer, who assured him that Rebekah's actions were a clear violation of the order, and that he should document everything.

But the calls and messages didn't stop. They came at all hours of the day and night, each one more threatening than the last. Rebekah's words were a venomous stream of accusations, threats, and promises of revenge.

One day, while scrolling through his social media feed, Martin froze, his blood running cold. Rebekah had posted a series of disturbing photos – images of Mariah, their faces distorted with malicious digital manipulation, accompanied by cryptic captions hinting at violence and despair.

He felt a surge of rage, his hands shaking as he reported the posts to the authorities. He knew Rebekah was unhinged, but this was a new level of depravity. She was using their daughter as a weapon, a pawn in her twisted game of revenge.

The following day, a notification popped up on his phone. Rebekah had tagged him in a new post. He clicked on it, his heart pounding in his chest.

It was a photo of their old apartment, the one they had shared before everything fell apart. A caption overlayed the image: "This is where it all began...and this is where it will end."

Martin's breath hitched in his throat. He recognized the implied threat, the chilling promise of retribution. He immediately called the police, his voice shaking as he explained the situation.

The officers arrived promptly, their faces grim as they reviewed the disturbing posts. They assured Martin that they would increase patrols around his home and advised him to be extra vigilant.

But the feeling of unease lingered, a constant shadow that followed him wherever he went. He installed additional security cameras, double-checked the locks on his doors and windows, and kept his gun close at hand.

He even considered sending Mariah to stay with his parents in Ohio, but the thought of being separated from her was unbearable. He couldn't let Rebekah win, couldn't let her drive a wedge between him and his daughter.

He tried to focus on his work, on his new life with Mariah. They went to the park, played games, and read stories together. He tried to create a sense of normalcy, of security, for his daughter's sake.

But the threat of Rebekah loomed over them, a dark cloud that refused to dissipate. Martin knew that he couldn't rest until she was stopped, until he and Mariah were truly safe.

One night, as he lay in bed, unable to sleep, he made a decision. He would not be a victim any longer. He would fight back, not with violence, but with the truth. He would expose Rebekah's lies, her manipulations, her dangerous instability. He would use his knowledge, his resources, his unwavering determination to protect his daughter.

He would not let Rebekah's darkness extinguish their light.

———

The sterile conference room at Robert Johnson's law office was a stark contrast to the turmoil raging within Martin. Sunlight streamed through the blinds, casting long, sharp shadows on the polished wooden table. Martin sat tensely, his hands gripping the armrests of his chair, his knuckles white. Across from him, Mr. Johnson, his attorney, reviewed the latest batch of evidence: a series of increasingly threatening text messages, the disturbing social media posts, and a chilling photo of their old apartment with a menacing caption.

"This is clearly escalating," Mr. Johnson said, his voice grave. "Rebekah's behavior is becoming more erratic, more unpredictable. We need to take immediate action to protect you and Mariah."

Martin nodded, his throat tightening. "I know," he said, his voice barely a whisper. "I'm terrified of what she might do next."

Mr. Johnson leaned forward, his gaze unwavering. "We need to strengthen the restraining order," he said. "We need to make it clear to the court that Rebekah is a danger to you and Mariah." Martin's eyes widened with a flicker of hope. "Can we do that?" he asked.

"Absolutely," Mr. Johnson replied. "We'll file a motion to modify the existing order, citing the recent escalation in her behavior. We'll also request that the court order her to undergo a psychological evaluation and a substance abuse assessment."

Martin nodded, a sense of relief washing over him. He had felt so powerless in the face of Rebekah's relentless harassment, but now, with the full force of the law behind him, he felt a glimmer of hope.

"What about the social media posts?" he asked. "Can we use those as evidence?"

Mr. Johnson nodded. "Absolutely. They're a clear indication of her instability and her intent to harm you. We'll present them to the judge as evidence of her escalating threats."

They spent the next hour discussing their strategy, reviewing the evidence, and preparing for the upcoming court hearing. Martin left the office feeling a renewed sense of determination. He would not let Rebekah intimidate him, would not allow her to control his life any longer. He would fight for his and Mariah's safety, no matter the cost.

In the days leading up to the hearing, Martintook every
precaution to ensure their safety. He installed additional security cameras around the house, changed the locks on all the doors, and rarely left the house without a trusted friend or family member watching Mariah. He even considered sending her to stay with his parents in Ohio, but the thought of being separated from her during this tumultuous time was unbearable.

He tried to shield Mariah from the growing tension, showering her with love and attention, filling their days with laughter and playful activities. But he could see the fear in her eyes, the questions that lingered unspoken. He knew that she sensed the danger, the underlying current of unease that permeated their lives.

The day of the hearing arrived, and Martin and Mr. Johnson entered the courthouse, their footsteps echoing in the marbled halls. The courtroom was filled with the familiar scent of stale coffee and antiseptic, a stark reminder of the sterile environment where justice was dispensed.

As they waited for the judge to enter, Martin's nerves tightened. He had never been one for confrontation, preferring to avoid conflict whenever possible. But now, he knew he had to stand his ground, to fight for his and Mariah's right to live a life free from fear.

The judge, a stern-faced woman with a reputation for fairness, entered the courtroom and called the case. Mr. Johnson presented their motion to modify the restraining order, meticulously detailing Rebekah's escalating threats and erratic behavior. He presented the social media posts as evidence, highlighting the disturbing nature of the content and the implicit threat they posed.

Rebekah's attorney argued that the posts were simply venting, a harmless expression of frustration. He portrayed Rebekah as a heartbroken mother who was simply trying to cope with the loss of her child.

Martin listened to the arguments with a growing sense of disbelief. He knew Rebekah's tactics, her ability to twist the truth and manipulate those around her. He watched as she sat beside her attorney, her face a mask of innocence, her eyes filled with crocodile tears.

But Judge Morrison was not swayed. After hearing both sides, she ruled in Martin's favor, granting his motion to modify the restraining order. She ordered Rebekah to undergo a psychological evaluation and a substance abuse assessment, and she extended the restraining order for an additional year.

As Martin left the courthouse, a wave of relief washed over him. He had won this battle, but he knew the war was far from over. Rebekah was not one to give up easily, and he would have to remain vigilant, always on guard against her next move.

But in that moment, as he held Mariah's hand tightly in his, he felt a glimmer of hope. He had taken a stand, he had fought for their safety, and he had won. He would not let Rebekah's darkness consume them. He would continue to fight, to protect his daughter, and to build a new life for them, a life filled with love, laughter, and the freedom to be themselves.

Chapter 15: A Mother's Betrayal

A thick tension hung in the air as Martin pulled into the driveway of his new home, a modest ranch nestled in a quiet cul-de-sac in Gilbert. The house, once a symbol of new beginnings, now felt tainted with unease. A nagging feeling tugged at his gut, a prickling sensation on the back of his neck, like an unseen predator lurking in the shadows.

Mariah's car seat sat empty in the back, a stark reminder of the constant juggling act of single parenthood. He had just dropped her off at Helen's for the weekend, a temporary respite from the looming threat of Rebekah's instability. He knew Helen adored having Mariah, and the time away would give Martin a chance to catch his breath.

He stepped out of the car, his keys jingling nervously in his hand. As he approached the front door, he noticed something amiss. The door was slightly ajar, a sliver of darkness peeking through the gap. A cold dread settled over him, his heart pounding against his ribs.

He cautiously pushed the door open, his eyes scanning the dimly lit hallway. Nothing seemed out of place, but the air hung heavy with an unsettling stillness. He moved through the house, his footsteps echoing in the silence, his senses on high alert.

He entered the bedroom, his gaze immediately drawn to the open gun safe. His blood ran cold. The safe was empty, the foam padding indented where his Glock and AR-15 had once rested. A wave of nausea washed over him as the realization hit him. Rebekah had been here. She had violated the restraining order, broken into his house, and stolen his guns.

A surge of adrenaline coursed through his veins, his mind racing with a thousand terrifying scenarios. What was she planning to do with the guns? Was she coming back? Was Mariah safe?

He grabbed his phone, his fingers trembling as he dialed 911. He explained the situation to the dispatcher, his voice strained with urgency. He gave them his address and a description of Rebekah, his words tumbling out in a rush of fear and anger.

As he waited for the police to arrive, he paced the living room, his mind a whirlwind of thoughts and emotions. He cursed himself for not being more vigilant, for leaving the house unguarded, even for a few hours. He had been so focused on protecting Mariah that he had neglected his own safety.

The arrival of the police brought a momentary sense of relief. He recounted the events to the officers, his voice shaking with barely suppressed rage. They took fingerprints, dusted for evidence, and promised to do everything they could to apprehend Rebekah.

But their reassurances did little to quell Martin's fear. He knew Rebekah was unhinged, capable of anything. The fact that she had stolen his guns, a clear violation of the restraining order, sent a chilling message. She was not going to give up easily.

He spent the rest of the day in a state of heightened anxiety, his mind racing with worst-case scenarios. He called Helen, his voice trembling as he explained what had happened. She assured him that Mariah was safe with her, but her voice betrayed her own fear and concern.

As the sun set, casting long shadows across the quiet street, Martin retreated to his bedroom. He sat on the edge of the bed, staring at the empty gun safe, his mind a battleground of conflicting emotions. He felt a deep sense of betrayal, a raw anger that simmered beneath the surface. How could Rebekah, the woman he had once loved, stoop so low? How could she jeopardize their daughter's safety in such a reckless and selfish way?

He also felt a profound sense of failure. He had vowed to protect Mariah, to shield her from the darkness that had consumed their lives. But he had failed. He had allowed Rebekah to violate their sanctuary, to steal the very weapons he had intended to use for their protection.

As he lay in bed that night, unable to sleep, he made a decision. He would not be a victim any longer. He would fight back, not with violence, but with the full force of the law. He would expose Rebekah's lies, her manipulations, her dangerous instability.

He would not rest until she was brought to justice, until he and Mariah were truly safe.

———

The harsh fluorescent lights of the police station interrogation room cast long shadows across Martin's face, accentuating the fatigue etched into his features. He sat across from Detective Lopez, a seasoned veteran with a world-weary demeanor and a piercing gaze that seemed to bore into his soul.

"We're doing everything we can, Mr. Reed," Lopez assured him, his voice a low rumble. "We've issued a warrant for Rebekah's arrest, and we're actively searching for her."

Martin nodded, his throat tight with barely suppressed rage. "Thank you, Detective," he said, his voice hoarse. "I just want her stopped. I want her to leave us alone."

Lopez leaned forward, his eyes fixed on Martin's face. "We need to establish a motive, Mr. Reed," he said. "Why do you think she stole your guns?"

Martin hesitated, a wave of disgust washing over him. He had been dreading this part, the inevitable questions that would force him to confront the ugly truth of his shattered marriage.

"She's...unstable," he finally managed, his voice barely a whisper. "She's been making threats, posting disturbing things online..."

He trailed off, unable to continue. The shame and humiliation of admitting his wife's instability to a stranger was almost unbearable.

Lopez nodded, his expression impassive. "We've seen the posts," he said. "They're certainly concerning. But we need more. Is there anything else you can tell us? Anything that might help us understand her state of mind?"

Martin closed his eyes, a painful memory surfacing from the depths of his subconscious. He saw Rebekah's face, twisted with rage, as she lunged at him with a knife. He heard her venomous words, the threats she had whispered in his ear.

He opened his eyes, his gaze meeting Lopez's. "She's been seeing someone," he said, his voice thick with disgust. "A man named
Alex."

Lopez raised an eyebrow. "Alex?"

Martin nodded. "I found a text message on her phone a few weeks ago," he explained. "It was clear they were having an affair."

Lopez's pen scratched against his notepad as he jotted down the information. "And this affair, it's still ongoing?" he asked.

Martin hesitated. "I...I don't know," he admitted. "I haven't seen any evidence of it recently, but..."

He trailed off, his mind reeling with a new wave of betrayal. The thought of Rebekah continuing her affair, even after everything that had happened, filled him with a sickening sense of revulsion.

Lopez leaned forward, his voice low and confidential. "Mr. Reed," he said, "it's important that you tell me everything you know. Any information, no matter how insignificant it may seem, could help us understand Rebekah's motives and locate her."

Martin nodded, steeling himself for the confession he was about to make. "I think she's still seeing him," he said, his voice barely a whisper. "I...I found a receipt in her purse the other day. It was from a hotel, a few towns over."

He paused, his cheeks burning with shame. "I didn't confront her about it," he admitted. "I was too...ashamed."

Lopez nodded understandingly. "I understand," he said. "This is a lot to process."

He leaned back in his chair, his expression thoughtful. "It seems like we have a clearer picture now," he said.

"Rebekah is clearly unstable, and she's motivated by jealousy and a desire for revenge. She may be trying to harm you, or even herself."

Martin's heart pounded in his chest. "What are you going to do?" he asked, his voice filled with fear.

"We're going to find her, Mr. Reed," Lopez assured him. "We'll do everything we can to bring her in safely, and to ensure that you and Mariah are protected."

Martin thanked him, a glimmer of hope flickering in his eyes. He knew that the road ahead would be long and difficult, but he also knew that he was not alone. He had the support of the police, his lawyer, and his loved ones. He would not let Rebekah's darkness consume him. He would fight back, protect his daughter, and reclaim his life.

———

The sharp beep of the security system echoed through the house as Martin punched in the code, disarming the newly installed alarm. The house, once a sanctuary of peace, now felt like a fortress under siege. Every creak and groan of the old building set his nerves on edge, every shadow seemed to harbor a lurking threat.

He had spent the day transforming his home into a high-tech security zone. Motion sensors guarded every entrance, surveillance cameras monitored the perimeter, and a reinforced steel door replaced the flimsy wooden one that had offered little resistance to Rebekah's intrusion.

As he moved through the house, checking and rechecking the locks, his heart pounded with a mixture of fear and resolve. He knew that Rebekah was out there, lurking in the shadows, her mind consumed by a twisted desire for revenge. He could feel her presence like a phantom limb, a constant reminder of the danger that surrounded him and his daughter.

He entered Mariah's room, the soft glow of her nightlight casting a comforting halo around her sleeping form. He tucked her blanket around her tiny shoulders, his heart swelling with a fierce protectiveness. He would never let Rebekah hurt her, never allow her to poison their lives with her toxic presence.

He returned to the living room, where he had set up a makeshift command center. His laptop glowed with the live feed from the security cameras, each screen a window into the world outside. He scanned the grainy images, his eyes searching for any sign of movement, any hint of danger.

He had become a prisoner in his own home, his every move dictated by fear and paranoia. He jumped at every unexpected sound, his hand instinctively reaching for the gun he now kept holstered at his hip.

He tried to distract himself with work, spending hours poring over cybersecurity reports, analyzing data, and developing new security protocols. But even as his mind grappled with complex problems, a part of him remained hyper-vigilant, constantly scanning the environment for potential threats.

He barely ate or slept, his body fueled by adrenaline and a relentless anxiety that gnawed at his soul. He had lost weight, his clothes hanging loose on his once-muscular frame. Dark circles had formed under his eyes, a testament to the sleepless nights spent worrying about Rebekah's next move.

He tried to maintain a semblance of normalcy for Mariah's sake, but his fear was palpable, a thick fog that permeated their lives. Mariah, perceptive beyond her years, sensed her father's unease, her own laughter becoming more subdued, her eyes often clouded with worry.

One evening, as Martin was reading Mariah a bedtime story, she looked up at him, her big blue eyes filled with concern. "Daddy, is the bad lady coming back?" she asked, her voice barely a whisper.

Martin's heart ached at her question. He had tried to shield her from the truth, to protect her from the ugliness of their situation.
But he knew he couldn't lie to her, not anymore.

He took a deep breath, his voice steady but gentle. "No, sweetheart," he said, stroking her hair. "The bad lady is not coming back. She's not allowed to come here anymore."

Mariah nodded, her eyes still filled with uncertainty. "But why did she take your guns, Daddy?" she asked. "Was she going to hurt us?"

Martin hesitated, unsure of how to answer. He didn't want to frighten her, but he also didn't want to lie. He decided to tell her a simplified version of the truth.

"Mommy was very sick," he said. "She did some bad things, and she needs help. But we're safe now, sweetheart. I promise."

Mariah snuggled closer to him, her tiny arms wrapped tightly around his neck. "I love you, Daddy," she whispered.

"I love you too, my little sunshine," Martin replied, his voice thick with emotion.

He held her close, his heart filled with a fierce determination to protect her, to shield her from the darkness that had threatened to consume their lives. He would not let Rebekah's madness win. He would fight for their future, for a life filled with love, laughter, and the freedom to be themselves.

Chapter 16: The Car Accident

The ringing phone shattered the peaceful silence of Helen's home. Martin jolted awake, his heart pounding as he fumbled for the receiver. It was the police. His blood ran cold as he heard the words "accident," "Rebekah," and "Mariah" tumble from the officer's mouth.

His mind raced, a chaotic symphony of fear and dread. He dressed frantically, his hands shaking as he buttoned his shirt. He mumbled a hasty explanation to Helen, who paled visibly upon hearing the news.

"I'll come with you," she insisted, her voice trembling.

They raced through the pre-dawn streets of Gilbert, the headlights of their car cutting through the darkness like a pair of accusing eyes. Martin's mind conjured images of twisted metal, shattered glass, and his precious daughter, her innocence forever marred by tragedy.

The scene at the accident site was a macabre ballet of flashing lights and grim-faced first responders. A mangled SUV lay on its side, its windows shattered, the air thick with the scent of gasoline and burnt rubber. Martin's heart lurched in his chest as he spotted a child's car seat lying amidst the wreckage.

He stumbled out of the car, his legs barely able to support him. Helen followed close behind, her hand gripping his arm for support. A police officer intercepted them, his face a mask of somber professionalism.

"Mr. Reed?" he asked, his voice gruff.

Martin nodded, his throat constricting with fear. "Where's my daughter?" he choked out.

The officer gestured towards an ambulance. "She's in there, sir.
Paramedics are checking her over, but she seems to be okay."

Relief washed over Martin like a tidal wave. He rushed towards the ambulance, his heart pounding with a mixture of joy and dread. He found Mariah strapped to a gurney, her eyes wide with fright, but otherwise unharmed.

He scooped her up in his arms, his body shaking with relief. "Daddy's here, sweetheart," he whispered, his voice thick with emotion. "Everything's going to be okay."

Mariah clung to him, her tiny arms wrapped tightly around his neck. She buried her face in his shoulder, her body trembling with silent sobs. Martin held her close, his tears mingling with hers, grateful that she was alive and unharmed.

He turned to the paramedic, his voice trembling. "What about Rebekah?"

The paramedic's expression was grim. "She's in critical condition, sir," he said. "She sustained multiple injuries, including head trauma and internal bleeding. We're doing everything we can, but..."

He trailed off, his words hanging heavy in the air. Martin's heart sank. Despite the relief of Mariah's safety, a wave of conflicting emotions washed over him. Anger, betrayal, and a lingering sense of guilt battled within him.

He watched as the paramedics loaded Rebekah into the ambulance, her body limp and lifeless. He couldn't help but wonder how it had come to this, how the woman he had once loved had become so lost in her own darkness.

Helen stood beside him, her eyes filled with tears. "This is all my fault," she whispered, her voice choked with guilt. "I should have seen the signs, I should have done something."

Martin reached out and took her hand, his voice gentle. "No, Helen," he said. "This is not your fault. Rebekah made her own choices. We have to focus on Mariah now, on protecting her and helping her heal."

They followed the ambulance to the hospital, their hearts heavy with uncertainty. The waiting room was a sterile, impersonal space, its silence punctuated only by the rhythmic beeping of medical equipment and the occasional hushed conversation.

Martin and Helen sat in silence, their hands clasped together, their eyes fixed on the double doors that led to the operating room. Hours passed, each minute stretching into an eternity.

Finally, a doctor emerged, his face grave. "Mrs. Reed is in stable condition," he said, "but she has a long road to recovery ahead of her. She'll need extensive surgery and rehabilitation."

Martin nodded, his mind numb with shock. He couldn't process the information, the surreal reality of Rebekah's life hanging in the balance.

He looked at Helen, her face pale and drawn. "What do we do now?" he asked, his voice barely a whisper.

Helen squeezed his hand, her eyes filled with determination. "We fight," she said. "We fight for Mariah, we fight for justice, and we fight for a better future."

———

The sterile scent of antiseptic and the muted beeps of medical equipment assaulted Martin's senses as he rushed through the sliding glass doors of the emergency room. Helen trailed behind him, her face pale and drawn, her grip on his arm tightening with each step.

"Please, God, let her be okay," Helen whispered, her voice trembling with barely contained fear.

Martin's heart pounded in his chest, a relentless drumbeat of anxiety and dread. He scanned the bustling waiting room, his eyes frantically searching for any sign of his daughter. A nurse, her face etched with concern, intercepted them.

"Mr. Reed?" she asked, her voice gentle but firm.

Martin nodded, unable to speak past the lump in his throat.

"I'm Nurse Martinez," she introduced herself. "Your daughter, Mariah, is being examined by the doctor. She seems to be okay, just a few minor scratches and bruises. But she's understandably shaken up."

Relief washed over Martin like a tidal wave, his knees buckling momentarily. He reached out to steady himself against a nearby wall, his hand trembling as he wiped away the tears that welled up in his eyes.

"Thank God," he whispered, his voice thick with emotion.

Helen let out a sob of relief, her body sagging against him. "Oh, thank God," she echoed, her voice muffled against his shoulder.

The nurse guided them to a private waiting room, a small, sterile space with vinyl chairs and a flickering fluorescent light. They sat in silence, their hands clasped together, their minds racing with a whirlwind of thoughts and emotions.

Martin's initial relief at Mariah's safety was quickly replaced by a surge of anger and resentment towards Rebekah. How could she be so reckless, so selfish, as to put their daughter's life in danger? The image of the mangled SUV, the shattered car seat, flashed through his mind, a chilling reminder of the fragility of life.

He felt a deep sense of betrayal, a raw anger that bubbled up from the depths of his soul. How could the woman he had once loved, the woman he had vowed to protect, inflict such pain and suffering on their family?

Helen, sensing his turmoil, reached out and squeezed his hand. "It's not your fault, Martin," she said, her voice soft and reassuring. "You did everything you could."

Martin shook his head, his voice thick with guilt. "I should have seen this coming," he said. "I should have protected her."

Helen shook her head, her eyes filled with compassion. "Don't blame yourself, dear," she said. "Rebekah is responsible for her own actions. We can't control her choices, but we can control how we react to them."

Her words offered little comfort to Martin. He was consumed by guilt, anger, and a deep sense of helplessness. He couldn't erase the trauma that Mariah had endured, the fear and confusion she must have felt as the car spun out of control.

He closed his eyes, his mind replaying the phone call from the police officer, the frantic drive to the hospital, the sight of the wreckage. He felt a wave of nausea wash over him, his stomach churning with a mix of anxiety and grief.

He opened his eyes, his gaze falling on Helen's face. She looked so fragile, so vulnerable. He knew that she was blaming herself for Rebekah's actions, but he couldn't allow her to carry that burden.

He reached out and took her hand in his, his voice filled with love and reassurance. "We'll get through this together, Helen," he said.
"We'll be strong for Mariah."

Helen nodded, tears streaming down her face. "I love her so much," she whispered, her voice choked with emotion. "I can't bear the thought of her being hurt."

Martin squeezed her hand, his heart aching for her. He knew that this was a turning point for their family, a moment of reckoning that would forever change their lives.

He would not let Rebekah's darkness win. He would fight for Mariah, for their future, for a life free from fear and pain. He would channel his anger and grief into a burning desire for justice, for a resolution that would protect his daughter and ensure that Rebekah would never again threaten their peace.

_____

The sterile hum of the hospital's fluorescent lights buzzed in Martin's ears, a discordant symphony to the chaos of his thoughts. He paced the narrow hallway outside the ICU, his eyes darting to the closed doors, his heart clenching with each muffled sound that filtered through.

Mariah, thankfully oblivious to the gravity of the situation, had been taken to the pediatric ward for observation. Helen, her eyes red-rimmed from crying, had gone with her, promising to keep Martin updated. Alone in the hallway, he felt the full weight of the day's events crashing down on him.

His wife, the woman he had once loved, lay unconscious in a hospital bed, her body broken and bruised, her future uncertain.

And his daughter, his innocent, precious Mariah, had been caught in the crossfire of Rebekah's self-destruction.

A sense of guilt gnawed at him, a persistent whisper in the back of his mind. Had he done enough to protect them? Could he have prevented this tragedy?

His thoughts were interrupted by the arrival of a stern-faced woman in a crisp business suit. She introduced herself as Ms. Jenkins, a caseworker from Child Protective Services.

"Mr. Reed," she said, her voice brisk and professional. "I'm here to talk to you about Mariah."

Martin's stomach churned with apprehension. He knew what this meant. CPS was here to assess the situation, to determine if Mariah was safe in his care.

They moved to a small, windowless office, its walls adorned with posters promoting child safety and well-being. Ms. Jenkins took a seat opposite Martin, her expression neutral as she opened a file.

"I understand that Mariah was involved in a car accident with her mother," she began, her voice devoid of emotion. "Can you tell me what happened?"

Martin recounted the events leading up to the accident, his voice shaking at times as he described Rebekah's erratic behavior, her threats, and the stolen guns. He detailed the restraining order, the escalating danger, and his growing fear for their safety.

Ms. Jenkins listened intently, her pen scribbling notes in her file. She asked probing questions about Rebekah's mental health history, her substance abuse, and her parenting abilities.

Martin answered honestly, his voice thick with emotion. He described Rebekah's struggles with depression and anxiety, her increasing reliance on medication, and her erratic mood swings. He spoke of the love he had once felt for her, the hope he had held onto for so long, and the devastating realization that she was no longer the woman he had married.

As he spoke, he felt a wave of shame wash over him. He had failed to protect his daughter, had allowed her to be exposed to the toxic environment of Rebekah's instability. He was a failure as a husband, as a father.

Ms. Jenkins, sensing his distress, offered a tissue. "This is not your fault, Mr. Reed," she said gently. "You are not responsible for your wife's actions."

Her words offered little comfort. Martin knew that he had played a role in this tragedy, that he had ignored the warning signs, that he had clung to hope when he should have acted sooner.

Ms. Jenkins continued her questioning, delving into the details of Martin's current living situation, his support system, and his plans for Mariah's care. He explained that he had moved in with his mother-in-law, Helen, who was a loving and supportive caregiver. He spoke of his job, his flexible schedule, and his unwavering commitment to providing for Mariah's needs.

After a lengthy interview, Ms. Jenkins closed her file, her expression thoughtful. "Mr. Reed," she said, "based on the information you have provided, I believe that Mariah is not safe in her mother's care at this time. We will be opening an investigation into Mrs. Reed's fitness as a parent. In the meantime, Mariah will remain in your custody."

Martin nodded, a wave of relief washing over him. He knew that this was the best decision for Mariah, the only decision that would ensure her safety and well-being.

He thanked Ms. Jenkins for her time and left the office, a renewed sense of purpose filling him. He would fight for his daughter, protect her from the darkness that had threatened to consume their lives. He would create a new life for them, a life filled with love, laughter, and the promise of a brighter future.

As he walked down the hospital corridor, his hand tightly gripping Mariah's, he knew that the road ahead would be long and arduous. But he also knew that he was not alone. He had the support of his family, his friends, and the unwavering love for his daughter to guide him through the darkness.

Chapter 17: Second Protection Order

The courtroom felt different this time. Not the suffocating tension of the custody hearing, but a steely resolve. Martin sat straighter, his jaw firm, the bruises on his face a stark testament to Rebekah's escalating violence. Beside him, Mr. Johnson, his attorney, exuded quiet confidence, his briefcase bulging with documented evidence of Rebekah's transgressions.

Across the aisle, Rebekah's presence was a storm cloud. Her eyes, once sparkling with life, were now dull and hollow, her face etched with a bitterness that chilled Martin to the bone. Her new attorney, a sharp-suited woman named Ms. Davis, radiated a cool, calculating energy.

The judge, a different one this time, a man with a no-nonsense demeanor, called the court to order. "Mr. Reed," he began, his voice echoing in the silent courtroom, "you have filed for a modification of the existing restraining order against your wife, Mrs. Reed. Please state your reasons."

Martin took a deep breath, his voice steady as he addressed the judge. "Your Honor, since the initial restraining order was issued, my wife's behavior has escalated significantly. She has violated the order multiple times, harassing me with threatening messages and calls, and even breaking into my home to steal my firearms."

He paused, his gaze briefly meeting Rebekah's before returning to the judge. "I fear for my safety and, more importantly, the safety of my daughter, Mariah. I believe that a more restrictive order is necessary to protect us from further harm."

Ms. Davis rose to her feet, her voice sharp as she countered Martin's claims. "Your Honor, my client is a grieving mother who has been unfairly separated from her child. Her actions, while perhaps misguided, are motivated by love and desperation."

Martin scoffed inwardly. Love? Desperation? These were the same twisted justifications Rebekah had used to excuse her abuse for months. He refused to be manipulated again.

Mr. Johnson, his voice a steady counterpoint to Ms. Davis's theatrics, presented the evidence: a stack of printed emails, text messages filled with vitriol and threats, and the police report detailing the break-in and theft of Martin's firearms.

"The evidence speaks for itself, Your Honor," Mr. Johnson stated calmly. "Mrs. Reed's actions demonstrate a clear disregard for the law and a blatant disregard for Mr. Reed and Mariah's safety. We urge the court to grant the motion for a modified restraining order with stricter terms."

The courtroom fell silent as the judge reviewed the evidence. Martin held his breath, his heart pounding in his chest. This was it, the moment of truth.

After what seemed like an eternity, the judge finally spoke. "Based on the evidence presented, I find that there is sufficient cause to modify the existing restraining order," he declared. "Mrs. Reed will be prohibited from any contact with Mr. Reed or Mariah, including phone calls, emails, text messages, or social media contact. She will also be prohibited from coming within 500 feet of their residence, workplace, or school."

A wave of relief washed over Martin, his shoulders sagging as the tension drained from his body. He had won. He had done everything he could to protect his daughter.

He glanced at Rebekah, who sat frozen in her chair, her face pale and expressionless. He felt a pang of sadness for the woman she had become, but he knew that he could not allow pity to cloud his judgment.

He turned to Mr. Johnson, his voice thick with emotion. "Thank you," he said. "Thank you for everything."

Mr. Johnson nodded, a rare smile gracing his lips. "You're welcome, Martin," he said. "You did the right thing."

As they left the courtroom, Martin felt a sense of vindication, a weight lifted from his shoulders. He had taken a stand against the darkness that had threatened to consume him, and he had emerged victorious. He knew that the battle was far from over, but he was ready to face whatever challenges lay ahead. He would protect Mariah, no matter the cost.

He looked down at his daughter, her tiny hand clasped tightly in his. She looked up at him, her eyes filled with trust and admiration. In that moment, Martin knew that he had made the right choice. He had chosen love, protection, and a future filled with hope.

———

The sterile white walls of the hospital room felt like a cage, trapping Rebekah in a prison of her own making. The lingering scent of disinfectant and the rhythmic beeps of the heart monitor served as a constant reminder of her broken body and shattered life. Her injuries from the car accident had healed, but the scars ran deeper than any physical wound.

She had lost everything. Her daughter, her husband, her home – all stripped away in the wake of her destructive spiral. The court's decision granting Martin sole custody of Mariah had been a devastating blow, a confirmation of her deepest fears. She was a failure as a mother, a monster who had endangered her own child.

Yet, even as the guilt and shame gnawed at her, a simmering rage bubbled beneath the surface. It was Martin's fault, she told herself. He had manipulated the system, turned everyone against her. He had painted her as a villain, a danger to their daughter. He had stolen her life, and she would make him pay.

As soon as she was discharged from the hospital, a plan began to form in her twisted mind. She would not accept defeat. She would not let Martin get away with this. She would fight for her daughter, no matter the cost.

Ignoring the stern warnings of her lawyer and the looming threat of legal consequences, she drove straight to Martin's new house, her heart pounding with a mixture of fear and determination. As she parked across the street, the sight of the newly installed security cameras and the reinforced steel door sent a shiver down her spine.

But she was not deterred. She had to see Mariah, to hold her in her arms, to tell her how much she loved her. She would not let Martin keep her daughter from her.

She dialed Martin's number, her hand trembling as she held the phone to her ear. It rang twice before he answered, his voice cold and distant.

"Rebekah, what do you want?" he asked, his tone laced with barely concealed disdain.

"I want to see Mariah," she said, her voice shaking with emotion.
"Please, Martin. I just want to see my daughter."

"You know you're not allowed to contact me," Martin replied. "You're violating the restraining order."

"I don't care," Rebekah retorted, her voice rising. "I'm her mother, and I have a right to see her."

"You lost that right when you endangered her life," Martin said, his voice hardening. "You're a danger to her, Rebekah. You need help."

Rebekah's rage exploded. "You're the one who needs help!" she screamed. "You're a manipulative bastard! You've turned everyone against me!"

She could hear Martin's sharp intake of breath on the other end of the line. "Don't you dare talk to me like that," he warned. "I'm calling the police."

"Go ahead," Rebekah sneered. "I'm not afraid of you. I'll get my daughter back, even if it's the last thing I do."

She hung up the phone, a triumphant smirk spreading across her face. She had rattled him, she could tell. He was scared, and that gave her a perverse sense of satisfaction.

She got out of the car and walked towards the house, her eyes fixed on the front door. She knew she couldn't get inside, but she wanted to make her presence known, to send a message to Martin that she would not be silenced, that she would not give up.

As she approached the door, she heard the sound of sirens in the distance. Her heart sank. She had been foolish, reckless, but she couldn't bear the thought of losing Mariah.

The police arrived moments later, their lights flashing, their sirens wailing. Rebekah stood frozen on the doorstep, her defiance giving way to a cold dread. She knew what was coming.

The officers approached her, their expressions grim. "Rebekah Reed?" one of them asked.

She nodded, her voice barely a whisper.

"You're under arrest for violating a restraining order," the officer said, his voice firm. "You have the right to remain silent. Anything you say can and will be used against you in a court of law." Rebekah's vision blurred as tears welled up in her eyes. She felt a sense of despair wash over her, a realization that she had lost everything. As the officers led her away, she turned and looked back at the house, her heart filled with a burning rage.

She would not give up. She would fight, she would claw her way back, and she would reclaim her daughter, no matter the cost.

The familiar scent of lavender and the soft glow of the Himalayan salt lamp in Dr. Grant's office offered a stark contrast to the harsh reality Martin had faced in the courtroom. He sank into the familiar leather armchair, his body heavy with exhaustion, his mind a whirlwind of conflicting emotions.

"Martin," Dr. Grant began, her voice a gentle balm to his frayed nerves, "I understand this has been an incredibly difficult time for you."

He nodded, his gaze fixed on the swirling patterns in the rug beneath his feet. "It's been a nightmare," he admitted, his voice thick with emotion. "I can't believe she would do something so reckless, so dangerous. She could have killed Mariah."

Dr. Grant leaned forward, her eyes filled with concern. "You're right," she said. "Her actions were inexcusable. But it's important to remember that you're not responsible for her choices. You did everything you could to protect Mariah."

Martin sighed, his shoulders slumping. "I know," he said, his voice barely a whisper. "But I can't help but feel guilty. What if I had done something differently? What if I hadn't left her?"

Dr. Grant reached out and gently squeezed his hand. "Those are normal feelings, Martin," she reassured him. "It's natural to second-guess yourself in situations like this. But it's important to remember that you made the best decision you could with the information you had at the time."

She paused, letting her words sink in. "Rebekah's actions are a reflection of her own struggles, not yours," she continued. "You cannot control her behavior, but you can control your own reactions to it."

Martin nodded, a glimmer of understanding dawning in his eyes. He had spent countless hours replaying the events of the past few months, searching for answers, blaming himself for the breakdown of his marriage. But Dr. Grant's words offered a different perspective, a way to reframe his experience.

"So, what do I do now?" he asked, his voice laced with desperation. "How do I cope with this trauma? How do I protect myself and Mariah from further harm?"

Dr. Grant smiled warmly. "That's what we're here for, Martin," she said. "We're going to work together to develop strategies for managing your anxiety, for protecting your mental well-being, and for creating a safe and healthy environment for you and Mariah." Over the next few weeks, Martin and Dr. Grant delved into the depths of his trauma, exploring the impact of Rebekah's abuse on his mental and emotional state. They discussed the physical symptoms of anxiety – the racing heart, the sweaty palms, the shortness of breath – and the emotional toll of living in constant fear.

Dr. Grant introduced Martin to a variety of coping mechanisms, including mindfulness meditation, deep breathing exercises, and progressive muscle relaxation. She taught him how to identify his triggers, to recognize the early warning signs of anxiety, and to intervene before it spiraled out of control.

They also discussed the importance of self-care, of prioritizing his own well-being in order to be a strong and supportive father for Mariah. Dr. Grant encouraged him to pursue activities that brought him joy and fulfillment, to reconnect with friends and family, and to find healthy outlets for his emotions.

As Martin began to implement these strategies, he noticed a gradual shift in his mindset. The constant anxiety that had plagued him began to lessen, replaced by a sense of calm and control. He started to sleep better, his appetite returned, and he found himself enjoying simple pleasures again – like reading a book, taking a walk in the park, or watching a movie with Mariah.

He also became more proactive in protecting himself and his daughter. He installed a security system in his mother-in-law's house, enrolled in a self-defense class, and developed a safety plan with his lawyer and the police.

He knew that the threat of Rebekah loomed large, a constant shadow that threatened to darken their lives. But he was no longer paralyzed by fear. He had the tools, the knowledge, and the support system to navigate the challenges ahead.

One evening, as he tucked Mariah into bed, he felt a wave of gratitude wash over him. He had come a long way since the darkest days of his marriage. He had faced his demons, confronted his past, and emerged stronger and more resilient.

He knew that the road to healing was not over, that there would be setbacks and challenges along the way. But he was no longer alone. He had Dr. Grant, his family, his friends, and his unwavering love for Mariah to guide him.

As he kissed his daughter goodnight, he whispered a silent prayer of gratitude. He was grateful for the second chance he had been given, the opportunity to create a new life filled with love, laughter, and the promise of a brighter tomorrow.

Chapter 18: Trust Shattered

The echoes of Mariah's laughter faded as Martin closed the door to her bedroom, the soft glow of her nightlight the only illumination in the otherwise darkened house. He moved to the living room, his footsteps muffled by the plush carpet, the silence amplifying the hollow ache in his chest.

Sinking onto the couch, he stared blankly at the flickering flames in the fireplace, their warmth failing to penetrate the chill that had settled over his soul. He reached for the worn leather journal on the coffee table, its pages filled with his raw emotions, his desperate attempts to make sense of the chaos that had become his life.

He flipped through the pages, his eyes scanning the entries, each one a snapshot of a different time, a different version of Rebekah. There was the Rebekah he had fallen in love with, the vibrant, passionate woman whose laughter had filled his world with sunshine. There was the Rebekah who had whispered sweet nothings in his ear, who had promised him a lifetime of love and happiness.

But there was also the Rebekah who had lashed out in anger, whose words had cut him deeper than any knife. There was the Rebekah who had manipulated and controlled him, who had isolated him from his loved ones and eroded his sense of self. There was the Rebekah who had shattered his trust, betrayed his love, and endangered their child.

As he read through the journal entries, a wave of grief washed over him, a mourning for the love that had been lost, the dreams that had been shattered. He had clung to the hope that Rebekah could be saved, that their love could conquer the darkness that had consumed her. But now, faced with the undeniable evidence of her betrayal and deceit, he realized that he had been living a lie.

He had been blinded by love, seduced by the illusion of happiness. He had ignored the red flags, the warning signs that had been there all along. He had allowed himself to be manipulated, controlled, and ultimately, destroyed.

He closed the journal, a single tear rolling down his cheek. He had loved Rebekah with all his heart, had given her everything he had. But his love had not been enough to save her from the demons that plagued her, the darkness that had twisted her soul.

He felt a deep sense of loss, a void that echoed through the empty chambers of his heart. He mourned the woman he had once known, the woman he had believed was his soulmate. He mourned the future they had planned together, the dreams they had shared.

But amidst the grief, there was also a sense of liberation. He was no longer bound by the chains of a toxic relationship, no longer a prisoner to Rebekah's whims and manipulations. He was free to rebuild his life, to create a new future for himself and Mariah.

He picked up a pen and began to write in the journal, his words flowing onto the page in a cathartic stream of consciousness. He wrote about the pain he had endured, the betrayal that had shattered his trust, the anger that simmered beneath the surface.

But he also wrote about the lessons he had learned, the hard-won wisdom that had emerged from the ashes of his broken marriage. He had learned that love is not enough, that trust and respect are the cornerstones of any healthy relationship. He had learned that he was stronger than he ever thought possible, that he could overcome even the most devastating of challenges.

He had learned that even in the darkest of times, there is always a glimmer of hope, a chance for redemption and renewal.

He wrote about his newfound commitment to self-care, to prioritizing his own well-being and the well-being of his daughter. He wrote about his determination to create a safe and loving home for Mariah, a place where she could grow and thrive, free from the shadow of her mother's instability.

He wrote about his dreams for the future, his hopes for a love that was true, a love that would cherish and respect him, a love that would never betray his trust.

As he closed the journal, a sense of peace settled over him. He had confronted his demons, acknowledged his pain, and embraced his resilience. He was ready to move forward, to create a new chapter in his life, a chapter filled with love, healing, and the promise of a brighter tomorrow.

———

The familiar scent of lavender incense filled Dr. Grant's office, a subtle undercurrent to the tension that hung in the air. Martin sat in the well-worn armchair, his posture rigid, his hands clenched tightly in his lap. His eyes, usually so full of warmth and compassion, were clouded with a deep-seated pain.

Dr. Grant, her gaze steady and empathetic, leaned forward. "Martin," she began, her voice soft and reassuring, "you've been through a lot. It's understandable that you're struggling with trust right now."

Martin nodded, his throat tight with emotion. "I don't know how to move forward," he confessed, his voice barely a whisper. "Every time I think about Rebekah, about what she did, I feel this... this rage, this sense of betrayal. But then, I also feel guilt, like it's somehow my fault."

He paused, his gaze drifting to the window, where a lone bird flitted across the azure sky. "I feel like I'm broken," he continued, his voice cracking. "Like I'll never be able to trust anyone again."

Dr. Grant nodded understandingly. "Trust is a fragile thing, Martin," she said. "It takes time and effort to build, and it can be shattered in an instant. But it's not impossible to rebuild."

She paused, letting her words sink in. "Let's talk about your past," she suggested. "Tell me about your childhood, your relationships, your experiences with trust."

Martin hesitated, his mind flashing back to a childhood filled with emotional neglect and conditional love. He spoke of his distant father, a workaholic who rarely showed affection. He talked about his mother, a woman who craved approval and validation, who often turned to Martin for emotional support.

He described his first serious relationship, a whirlwind romance with a woman who had cheated on him repeatedly, leaving him heartbroken and disillusioned. He spoke of the pattern that had emerged in his subsequent relationships, his tendency to attract women who were emotionally unavailable or manipulative.

As he spoke, a sense of clarity began to emerge. He realized that his trust issues were not a new phenomenon, but a deeply ingrained pattern that had roots in his childhood experiences. He had sought out relationships that mirrored the dysfunctional dynamics of his family, unconsciously seeking to recreate the familiar pain and neglect.

"It's not your fault, Martin," Dr. Grant reassured him. "These patterns were established long before you met Rebekah. But now that you're aware of them, you can begin to change them."

She explained how his childhood experiences had shaped his beliefs about love and relationships, how his need for validation had led him to make unhealthy choices. She helped him to understand that he was not responsible for Rebekah's actions, that her betrayal was a reflection of her own struggles, not his shortcomings.

"You deserve to be loved, Martin," she said, her voice filled with warmth and compassion. "You deserve to be in a healthy, fulfilling relationship. But in order to find that, you need to heal the wounds of your past, to learn to trust yourself and others."

Martin nodded, a glimmer of hope flickering in his eyes. He knew that the road to healing would be long and arduous, but he was determined to walk it. He would not let the trauma of his past define him.

Dr. Grant suggested a series of exercises and techniques to help Martin rebuild his trust. She encouraged him to start small, to focus on building trust with himself first, then gradually extending that trust to others.

She taught him how to set healthy boundaries, to communicate his needs clearly, and to recognize the red flags of toxic relationships. She encouraged him to surround himself with supportive people, people who would lift him up and encourage him on his journey to healing.

As the session drew to a close, Martin felt a sense of empowerment he hadn't felt in a long time. He had gained valuable insights into his past, his patterns, and his potential for growth. He knew that the road ahead would be challenging, but he was no longer afraid. He was ready to face the future, to embrace the possibility of love and trust once again.

———

The rhythmic screech of the saw blade cutting through wood filled the small garage, a surprisingly soothing counterpoint to the chaos that had been Martin's life. Sawdust swirled in the air, clinging to his hair and clothes, a tangible reminder of the physicality of this new endeavor.

Woodworking had started as a suggestion from his therapist, a way to channel his pent-up emotions into something constructive. Martin had always been a man of action, his FBI training ingrained in him a need for control and precision. But the emotional wreckage of his marriage had left him feeling adrift, his sense of agency shattered.

The first time he had stepped into the local woodworking shop, the scent of freshly cut timber and the sight of tools gleaming under the fluorescent lights had stirred something within him. It was a primal instinct, a connection to a simpler time, a world where problems were solved with hands and tools, not words and therapy sessions.

He had signed up for a beginner's class, his initial clumsiness and uncertainty a stark contrast to his usual confidence. But as he learned the basics – how to measure and cut wood, how to use a plane and a chisel, how to join pieces together – a sense of calm began to wash over him.

The act of creating something tangible with his hands, of transforming raw materials into something beautiful and functional, was incredibly therapeutic. It demanded his full attention, pushing aside the intrusive thoughts and anxieties that plagued him.

As he worked, his mind would quiet, the world narrowing down to the feel of the wood beneath his fingers, the smooth glide of the plane, the satisfying thunk of the hammer. He found himself losing track of time, the hours melting away as he focused on the task at hand.

He started with small projects: a simple birdhouse for Mariah, a rustic shelf for his new apartment, a handcrafted cutting board for
Helen. Each completed project brought a sense of accomplishment, a tangible reminder of his own strength and resilience.

One weekend, he decided to tackle a more ambitious project – a wooden toy chest for Mariah. He spent hours sketching out designs, meticulously measuring and cutting the wood, and carefully assembling the pieces. He sanded the rough edges, stained the wood a warm cherry hue, and added decorative accents with a wood burner.

As he put the finishing touches on the toy chest, a wave of pride washed over him. He had created something beautiful, something that would bring joy to his daughter for years to come. It was a tangible symbol of his love for her, a testament to his ability to create and nurture, even in the face of adversity.

He presented the toy chest to Mariah, her eyes widening with delight as she ran her fingers over the smooth wood and admired the intricate carvings. She immediately began filling it with her favorite toys, her laughter filling the apartment with a warmth that had been absent for far too long.

Martin watched her with a smile, his heart overflowing with love. He had found a new passion, a new way to express himself and connect with his daughter. He had rediscovered a sense of joy and accomplishment, a reminder that he was more than just a victim of circumstance.

He continued to devote his evenings and weekends to woodworking, his projects becoming more ambitious and complex. He built a bookshelf for his growing collection of literature, a coffee table for the living room, and even a custom-made crib for Mariah.

With each project, he honed his skills, his confidence growing with each successful completion. He learned to embrace the imperfections, the knots and blemishes that added character to the wood, just as his own scars and imperfections added depth to his soul.

He found a community of fellow woodworkers at the local shop, a group of men and women who shared his passion for the craft. They exchanged tips and techniques, offered encouragement and support, and created a space where Martin could be himself, free from the judgment and expectations of the outside world.

Woodworking became more than just a hobby for Martin. It was a form of therapy, a way to process his emotions, to heal his wounds, and to reconnect with his inner strength. It was a tangible reminder that he was capable of creating beauty, of building something meaningful from the wreckage of his past.

As he stood in his garage, the scent of sawdust and wood stain filling the air, he felt a sense of peace he had not known in a long time. He was no longer defined by the trauma he had endured, but by the resilience he had found within himself. He was a survivor, a creator, a man who was slowly but surely rebuilding his life, one piece of wood at a time.

Chapter 19: Building a Safer Future

The waiting room of the family therapist's office was a kaleidoscope of emotions. Children's drawings adorned the walls, a testament to the resilience of the human spirit, yet the underlying tension in the air was palpable. Martin sat beside Mariah, his arm wrapped protectively around her small frame. Her fingers fidgeted with the hem of her dress, her eyes darting nervously around the room.

Martin, noticing her anxiety, squeezed her hand reassuringly. "It's okay, sweetheart," he whispered, his voice a soothing balm against the sterile hum of the air conditioner. "We're in this together."

Mariah nodded, her lower lip trembling slightly. She was a resilient child, having weathered more emotional storms in her short life than most adults endure in a lifetime. But the scars of her mother's abuse ran deep, leaving her with a lingering sense of unease and a fear of the unknown.

The door to the therapist's office opened, and a warm smile greeted them. Dr. Emily Collins, a petite woman with kind eyes and a calming presence, ushered them into her office.

The room was a sanctuary of soft colors and gentle lighting, a stark contrast to the harsh reality of their lives. Bookshelves lined the walls, their titles promising solace and healing. A plush rug covered the floor, inviting them to shed their shoes and sink into its comforting embrace.

Dr. Collins settled into her armchair, her gaze shifting between Martin and Mariah. "Welcome," she said, her voice soft and inviting. "I'm so glad you're here."

She turned to Mariah, her smile widening. "Hello, Mariah," she said. "I'm Dr. Collins. It's so nice to meet you."

Mariah, her shyness momentarily forgotten, offered a tentative smile in return.

Dr. Collins turned back to Martin. "Martin, I understand that you and Mariah have been through a lot," she said, her voice laced with empathy. "I'm here to help you both navigate this difficult time and find a path towards healing."

Martin nodded, his throat tightening with emotion. He had been apprehensive about bringing Mariah to therapy, worried about exposing her to further trauma. But he knew that it was a necessary step, a chance for them to address the unspoken wounds that lingered beneath the surface.

Dr. Collins began by asking Martin about the events of the past few months, the custody battle, Rebekah's erratic behavior, and the impact it had had on their lives. Martin spoke openly and honestly, his voice at times choked with emotion, his words a testament to the pain and betrayal he had endured.

Mariah listened quietly, her eyes wide with a mixture of sadness and understanding. She had heard bits and pieces of her parents' story, but this was the first time she had heard the full truth, the unvarnished reality of her mother's illness and the devastating consequences it had wrought upon their family.

Dr. Collins then turned to Mariah, engaging her in a gentle conversation about her feelings. She asked her how she felt about her mommy, about the changes in their lives, about the fears and anxieties that kept her awake at night.

Mariah, hesitant at first, slowly began to open up. She spoke of her sadness at not seeing her mother, her confusion about why her parents couldn't live together anymore, and her fear that her mother might never get better.

Martin listened to his daughter's words with a heavy heart. He had tried to shield her from the pain, to protect her from the harsh realities of their situation. But he realized now that she needed to be heard, to have her feelings acknowledged and validated.

Dr. Collins gently guided the conversation, helping Martin and Mariah to communicate with each other in a safe and supportive environment. She taught them techniques for expressing their emotions, for listening to each other with empathy, and for working together to overcome their shared trauma.

As the session progressed, a sense of warmth and connection began to fill the room. Martin and Mariah shared stories, laughter, and tears. They spoke of their hopes for the future, their dreams of a life filled with love and happiness.

By the end of the session, Martin felt a renewed sense of hope. He had taken a crucial step towards healing, not only for himself but also for his daughter. He knew that the road ahead would be long and challenging, but he was no longer alone. He had Mariah by his side, and they had each other's love and support to guide them through the darkness.

_____

The low hum of the air conditioning unit blended with the soft lullaby playing from Mariah's room. The apartment, once echoing with the chilling silence of his solitude, now brimmed with the warmth of a home – albeit a temporary one. Martin sat at the small kitchen table, his laptop open, his fingers flying across the keyboard.

After weeks of late-night applications and countless interviews, a sense of accomplishment washed over him as he hit 'send' on his final email. It was an acceptance letter for a position as a Senior Cybersecurity Analyst at a renowned tech firm in Scottsdale. The salary was more than generous, the benefits package comprehensive, and most importantly, the company culture aligned with his values.

He leaned back in his chair, a deep exhale escaping his lips. For the first time in months, he felt a glimmer of hope. This job offered more than just financial security; it was a chance to rebuild his career, to utilize his skills for a greater purpose, to provide a stable and fulfilling life for Mariah.

He imagined a future where he could afford a house with a backyard for Mariah to play in, a place where she could grow up safe and loved. He envisioned taking her on vacations, exposing her to new experiences, and providing her with the opportunities he had never had.

But beyond the material benefits, the job offered a sense of validation, a reaffirmation of his worth and expertise. After months of feeling battered and broken by Rebekah's relentless abuse, he craved the feeling of accomplishment, the sense of purpose that came with making a meaningful contribution to society.

He closed his laptop, a smile tugging at his lips. He walked to Mariah's room, his heart swelling with love as he watched her sleep, her tiny chest rising and falling rhythmically. He gently tucked a stray curl behind her ear, his touch featherlight.

He knew that the road ahead would be challenging. The legal battles with Rebekah were far from over, and the emotional scars of their toxic marriage would take time to heal. But for the first time in a long time, he felt a sense of optimism, a belief that he and Mariah could overcome any obstacle, together.

The next morning, Martin woke up with a renewed sense of purpose. He dressed in his best suit, a stark contrast to the casual attire he had adopted in recent months. As he tied his tie, he caught a glimpse of himself in the mirror. He looked different, more confident, his eyes no longer clouded with the shadow of fear and doubt.

He picked up Mariah, who was babbling excitedly in her crib, her arms reaching out for him. He dressed her in a matching pink outfit, her giggles filling the room with a contagious joy.

He drove them to Helen's house, where he shared the good news about his new job. Helen, her eyes sparkling with pride, embraced him tightly.

"I knew you could do it, Martin," she said, her voice thick with emotion. "You're a strong and capable man. You and Mariah deserve all the happiness in the world."

Martin thanked her, his heart filled with gratitude for her unwavering support. He knew that he wouldn't have made it this far without her.

As he drove to his first day at the new job, a sense of anticipation filled him. He was ready to embrace this new chapter in his life, to build a brighter future for himself and his daughter. He would work hard, excel in his career, and create a legacy that Mariah could be proud of.

The gleaming office building, a towering monolith of glass and steel, represented a world far removed from the darkness of his past. As he stepped through the revolving doors, he felt a surge of adrenaline, a sense of excitement mingled with a healthy dose of trepidation.

He was greeted by his new colleagues, their friendly smiles and welcoming words easing his initial anxiety. He quickly settled into his new role, his expertise and experience proving invaluable to the company.

His days were filled with challenging tasks, his mind constantly engaged in solving complex problems. He found himself working late into the night, fueled by a desire to prove himself, to excel in his field, to create a secure future for his daughter.

In the evenings, he would return to Helen's house, exhausted but fulfilled. He would spend time with Mariah, playing games, reading stories, and simply enjoying her infectious laughter.

He cherished these moments, savoring the warmth and love that filled their small, makeshift home. He knew that he had been given a second chance, a chance to create a life that was truly his own, a life free from fear and pain.

He would not waste it.

The sun beat down on Martin's face, a warmth that he welcomed as a counterpoint to the chill that had lingered in his soul for far too long. He watched Mariah chase butterflies through the wildflowers, her infectious giggles filling the air with a melody of joy. The park was their sanctuary, a haven of green grass, towering trees, and the carefree laughter of children.

He had chosen this park specifically for its serenity. Nestled away from the bustling city center, it was a hidden gem, a place where time seemed to slow down, where worries and anxieties faded into the background.

As he watched Mariah twirling through the meadow, her sundress swirling around her like a vibrant flower, a sense of peace washed over him. He had been through hell and back, his life shattered by betrayal and violence. But here, in this moment, surrounded by the beauty of nature and the innocence of his daughter, he felt a glimmer of hope, a renewed sense of purpose.

He had fought tooth and nail to protect Mariah, to shield her from the darkness that had threatened to consume their lives. He had endured court battles, sleepless nights, and the constant fear of Rebekah's unpredictable behavior. But through it all, he had emerged stronger, more resilient, his love for his daughter his guiding light.

He had learned to forgive, not for Rebekah's sake, but for his own. He had let go of the anger and resentment that had poisoned his heart, choosing instead to focus on the present, on building a brighter future for himself and Mariah.

He had rediscovered the joy of simple pleasures, the beauty of nature, the power of human connection. He had found solace in his work, in his newfound faith, in the love and support of his family and friends.

He had also found love again, a tentative, hesitant love that was slowly but surely blossoming with Sarah. Their relationship was a stark contrast to the tumultuous chaos of his marriage to Rebekah. It was built on trust, respect, and a shared commitment to healing and growth.

As Mariah ran back to him, her arms outstretched, her face beaming with excitement, Martin scooped her up, twirling her around until they were both dizzy with laughter. He held her close, inhaling the sweet scent of her hair, his heart overflowing with love.

"Daddy, look!" Mariah exclaimed, pointing towards a colorful kite soaring high in the sky.

Martin followed her gaze, his eyes tracing the kite's graceful arc against the azure sky. He saw it as a symbol of their own journey, their ascent from the depths of despair towards a brighter future.

They spent the rest of the afternoon exploring the park, their laughter echoing through the trees. They built sandcastles in the sandbox, fed the ducks at the pond, and chased each other through the winding paths.

As the sun began to set, casting long shadows across the grass, Martin and Mariah sat on a bench overlooking the lake. The air was filled with the gentle chirping of crickets and the distant sound of children's laughter.

Mariah snuggled close to Martin, her head resting on his shoulder. "I love you, Daddy," she whispered.

"I love you too, sweetheart," Martin replied, his voice thick with emotion. "More than anything in the world."

He looked out at the horizon, the setting sun painting the sky in a breathtaking array of colors. He knew that the future was uncertain, that there would be challenges and obstacles ahead. But he also knew that he was not alone. He had Mariah by his side, their love a constant source of strength and inspiration.

Together, they would face whatever life threw their way, with courage, determination, and unwavering hope. They had overcome unimaginable challenges, and they would continue to rise, to thrive, to create a life filled with love, laughter, and the unwavering belief that even in the darkest of times, there is always light.

Milton Keynes UK
Ingram Content Group UK Ltd.
UKHW020050260824
447288UK00011B/337